ZEINA
STARBORN
and the SKY WHALE

D1341209

ZEINA STARBORN

and the SKY WHALE

HANNAH DURKAN

Hodder
Children's
Books

ORION CHILDREN'S BOOKS

First published in Great Britain in 2022 by Orion Children's Books

1 3 5 7 9 10 8 6 4 2

A CIP catalogue record for this book
is available from the British Library.

ISBN 978 1 510 10959 9

Printed and bound in Great Britain by Clays Ltd, Elcograf S.p.A.

The paper and board used in this book are from well-managed
forests and other responsible sources.

Orion Children's Books
An imprint of
Hachette Children's Group
Part of Hodder & Stoughton
Carmelite House
50 Victoria Embankment
London EC4Y 0DZ

An Hachette UK Company
www.hachette.co.uk

www.hachettechildrens.co.uk

To everyone who believed in me
when I couldn't believe in myself.

CHAPTER 1

The beams of two bright headlamps cut through the mist and shadows of that August afternoon and for once Zeina was glad for the smog. Had it not been so thick, she wouldn't have had time to hide. Gasping through her respirator mask, she ducked behind one of the crumbling statues that surrounded the imposing building and watched as the automobile came to a halt.

'Hurry up, Flora! There's no time for your dawdling today!'

The shrill voice of Mrs Hogwood made Zeina wince. She watched a frazzled maid scramble from the car, her arms sagging under a tower of boxes.

Mrs Hogwood waited for her door to be opened by the navy-capped chauffeur, before carefully adjusting her respirator mask and stepping out empty-handed into the haze. She dusted a smudge of soot from her crisp white gloves and straightened a particularly ugly hat. As always, she wore an

1

expression of disdain, her thin lips pinched and her beak-like nose raised in the air, as if there were a bad smell beneath it.

'The smog is awful today,' she snapped, as if it were somehow the chauffeur's fault.

'That it is, ma'am,' coughed the old man behind his own mask.

She gestured angrily towards the two whirring fans secured above the entrance to Willoughby Towers.

'I shall never get used to that infernal racket!' Her piercing cry rose above the din. 'What a mess! They completely ruin the facade!'

Zeina wasn't sure exactly what a "facade" was but agreed that the deafening fans – each easily the size of an airship propeller – were quite unbearable. They must have been working at full capacity.

Every building in Ravenport had fans which worked day and night in an attempt to clear the streets of the thick pollution that covered the city. Despite this, it had been many years since anyone had been able to step outside without their respirator mask.

Willoughby Towers was certainly the grandest building in all of Ravenport. Zeina had seen drawings of when it was first built – fifty floors of gleaming golden stone with high, arched windows separated by ornately carved columns and surrounded on all sides by immaculate gardens. Even now,

2

with its towering exterior blackened from ore fumes, cracked stone cherubs leering down through gap-toothed smiles, and lobby windows boarded shut against the noxious fumes, Zeina had to agree it was still pretty impressive. You couldn't see all the way to the top anymore, of course; looking up from the street outside, most of the building was completely obscured by thick, grey clouds.

For the people living inside Willoughby Towers, and the hundreds of tower blocks just like it across the Eastern Continent, life was a tale of two halves. *Belows* lived in the cramped, gloomy apartments below the city smog-line. Belows couldn't afford fine clothes or food or airship travel. Belows worked hard to survive. But for the other half, life was full of perks. Perks like the uniformed doorman who was now rushing to open the door for Mrs Hogwood. Unlike Zeina and other Belows, *Aboves* were permitted to use the grand entrance lobby and its golden electric lift. Aboves could afford the luxurious apartments, safely above the smog, on floors thirty and above. Aboves even had windows – ones they could actually open to breathe in the bright, clear air above the smog-line.

Zeina imagined Mrs Hogwood gazing out appreciatively from her window on floor forty-five, waving at the fine ladies and gentlemen of Ravenport travelling block to block in their airships. She also imagined how much Mrs Hogwood would

3

enjoy thinking about all the Belows stuck in that eternal murky twilight beneath her.

Zeina breathed a sigh of relief when, after a torrent of barked orders and complaints, Mrs Hogwood finally bustled into the building. When Zeina was quite sure the awful woman was safely inside, she darted out from behind the stone leg of Sir Phineas Bartholomew (Innovator of the Upper Atmosphere Airship), only to collide with someone else.

CRASH, BANG, THUD. Each dropped what they were carrying and fell to the ground with a yelping, cursing clatter.

'Why don't you look where you're going?' Zeina yelled as she disentangled her limbs from the boy's.

'What? I ... But *you* ran into *me*!' he replied. The boy was covered in so much mud that Zeina didn't immediately make out who it was. While he lay there dazed, she scrambled to pick up the array of objects that had fallen from her backpack – a rusted kitchen pan, a moth-eaten book, a selection of cogs and wires, a broken pocket watch and a number of smashed monocles.

The boy attempted to get to his feet, sinking back to the ground when he noticed the drops of red on the cobblestones. Beneath the blood from a deep gash on his eyebrow and the mud on his face, Zeina suddenly noticed the distinctive copper hair, fine features, flushed cheeks and large eyes, steel-blue. Her heart sank.

4

'Ah! It's you! And you're bleeding!' she exclaimed, rooting around in her pocket for a handkerchief and pressing it against his brow.

'Who . . . Who are you?'

This made Zeina bristle. He had seen her just as many times as she had seen him and yet *he* had no idea who *she* was. This was just like Aboves; people like Zeina were merely part of the scenery – completely forgettable.

'Who am I? NOBODY, that's who!' She knew she could get into trouble for talking to him this way. After all, he was technically her father's employer.

'Um, I'm Jackson. Jackson Willoughby.' He held out his hand, which she ignored.

'I know,' she said, gesturing to the plaque above the steps where, in golden lettering, was carved 'WILLOUGHBY TOWERS'.

'I'm sorry. Have we . . . met before?' he asked tentatively.

She laughed again. 'Only about a hundred times.'

'What? I'm sorry. Maybe I don't recognise you because of all the, erm . . . slime.'

This enraged Zeina – it wasn't her fault she'd fallen into the bog at the city dump. People like Jackson would never understand what it was like to have to go rummaging through the mountains of stuff Aboves threw away for the things you needed. Their cast-offs were her treasures. She swung her backpack on with a clank and removed her respirator mask, revealing a perfectly clean oval of nose, mouth, skin and freckles.

'Oh, I see. First you don't remember me and now you're trying to say I'm dirty?' She gave an exasperated snort. 'You're all the same. People like *you* never bother to remember people like *me*. Nope, you're just not worth noticing unless you're Queen La-de-da or Sir What's-It the Third, an owner of a fleet of airships, decked out in the latest fancy clothes . . .' She halted, noticing the state of Jackson's own clothes. As well as being completely covered in mud, the cuff of his jacket was torn and there were two missing silver buttons, not to mention the blood now dripping down from his eyebrow on to his collar. Zeina gulped, falling silent. No doubt she would be blamed for this too. Maybe it was for the best that he didn't recognise her.

Jackson scrambled to his feet.

'I . . . erm . . . had a little accident . . . on my velocycle,' he explained. He bent down to pick up his cycling machine where it lay in a twisted heap. It was covered in deep scratches down one side, the handlebars were scuffed and the front wheel was bent out of shape. 'I came off trying to beat my speed record round the old athletics track. I'm getting ready for the try-outs for the Ravenport Racers. You a fan?'

Zeina rolled her eyes. Everyone in Ravenport – Aboves

and Belows alike – supported the velocycle team. On match days, she and her father would take the packed cargo train right across the city, past the clanking, billowing factories, the scrapyards and the abandoned ore mines, right to the very edge of town where the Ravenport Racers's stadium was. She assumed Jackson Willoughby travelled to matches in one of his many airships.

'Yeah,' she answered coolly. 'I've got a signed poster of Franklyn Beaumont.'

'Oh, really? He's my favourite too,' said Jackson brightly. 'I've got one of him holding the Eastern Continent Cup, and last year's Ravenport Racers team photo, *and* this really cool one to celebrate when he won Player of the Year three years running.'

Zeina scowled at him.

'Don't you lot have your own rooftop parks?' she asked. 'Why are you skulking around the abandoned athletics track? Surprised you could see a hand in front of your face down there!'

'Well, I was trying to avoid my housekeeper, Mrs Hogwood. You see, she—'

'Urgh, Hoggy.' Zeina pretended to throw up in a nearby bush. 'I was hoping for a ride home in your fancy lift but Hoggy ruined all that. Can't risk it now she's on the prowl.'

'Can't you just come in with me?'

Zeina stared at him, incredulous. Was Jackson making a cruel joke or was he just so ignorant that he didn't get it? She decided on the latter. The lift attendant, Maxwell, would almost certainly lose his job if Mrs Hogwood caught her in the Above lift again. Now she was back, Zeina had no choice but to haul herself up all fifty floors in the rickety service lift, to the airship platform, right at the very top of Willoughby Towers.

'*Me?* Go in *there* with *you*? Don't be ridiculous,' she sighed, picking up the twisted velocycle and handing it to Jackson. 'S'pose you've got a servant or something that'll fix this for you.'

'Actually, I'll fix it myself,' said Jackson defensively.

Zeina raised one eyebrow. She doubted very much that that was true.

'It is beautiful,' she said, mesmerised, her hand outstretched towards the shining titanium frame. 'I'd do anything for my own velocycle.' She cursed herself – why had she said that out loud?

Zeina presumed Jackson had about ten velocycles; he could quite easily give her this one and probably wouldn't even notice it was gone.

'Well, you could have a go on this one, once it's fixed. If you want?' he added tentatively. 'We could meet up one day on the athletics track?'

For a moment she was taken aback by this gesture. Her heart lifted, but only for a second. He was making fun of her again, she was sure of it. And even if he wasn't, the thought of her and Jackson Willoughby velocycling together around the athletics track was quite one of the most ridiculous things she had ever heard.

'Nah, I don't think so, rich boy. I've got better things to do than mess about on some fancy velocycle. Some of us have work to do.'

And with that she turned away from Jackson's confused, dirty face and ran – a clanking cloud of dust disappearing into the smog-filled gardens from which she had come.

CHAPTER 2

J ackson waited, ear pressed up against the imposing door of carved mahogany. He had to time opening the door to the Willoughby apartment very carefully if he was going to reach his room safely and change out of his ruined clothes before Mrs Hogwood came looking for him.

His parents, as always, were holidaying somewhere in the Upper Atmosphere. He tried to remember where they were this time. Staying on that new sky whale hotel, the Blossomwell? No, touring the Northern Continent for the fourth time in their private airship, the *Golden Eagle* – that was it.

In the absence of his parents, Mrs Hogwood was ultimately responsible for him and took her duties *very* seriously indeed. He had been under strict instructions to stay in his room and study his copy of *The Sky Whale: A Natural History* while she completed her daily errands.

The clipped sound of her heels across the parquet floor

faded. Now or never. He removed his muddy boots and opened the door, tiptoeing carefully inside before gently shutting it behind him. Boots in hand, he turned towards the West Wing, creeping warily down the corridor that led to his room. He could actually see his bedroom door when he heard a cough behind him.

'What IN HEAVENS do you think you are doing?'

He turned, a shrill shriek filling his ears as Mrs Hogwood saw the full extent of his appearance.

'WHAT IN THE WORLD?! Just LOOK at the STATE of you!' Mrs Hogwood was standing in the trail of brown gloop that had dripped from his boots. Her face was purple, her hand clasping at her frilled collar. 'You've been out on that INFERNAL CONTRAPTION again, haven't you? HAVEN'T YOU?' She didn't wait for him to answer, striding over and grabbing his chin to look more closely at his eyebrow. 'WHAT have you done to yourself?' She let go of his chin roughly and flung both arms in the air with exasperation. 'And with your party only a week away! The physician will have to be called. We can't have your uncle seeing you looking like a COMMON THUG!'

'Oh, Mrs Hogwood, you know I really don't need a party.' Jackson had said this on numerous occasions over the past few months. He hated his annual birthday bash and this year would be even worse because it was his

11

twelfth – his last one in Ravenport before starting his apprenticeship with his uncle on the Willoughbys' sky whale hotel.

Aboves were flying in from all over the four continents for his birthday party, and his Uncle Hamilton and awful cousin Herbert were coming down; that's why Hogwood was in even more of a flap than usual.

'Don't be ridiculous. You *must* have a party! I can't imagine why you wouldn't want one, ungrateful boy!'

Jackson sighed, knowing full well there was no point in arguing.

'Now, go change out of those clothes at once. Your tutor has told me that you have an ENORMOUS amount of studying to do for you to have ANY chance of passing your exams. It won't be long before the responsibility of running that whale hotel falls to you, Master Jackson. And one day you'll be head of the WHOLE family! You MUST take your studies more seriously.'

'Yes, Mrs Hogwood,' Jackson replied, eyes down, teeth clenched for fear he would say something else entirely. He tucked the twisted velocycle behind his back.

She stalked off in a bustle of skirts, barking for Flora. 'Come and clean up this disgraceful mess RIGHT AWAY!'

His room was the only place Jackson felt truly at home. He walked past his desk – textbook still open at the same page it had been that morning – and straight to his wardrobe. Throwing it open, he pushed the layers of rich, heavy garments to one side, revealing his collection of velocycles and tools. He selected what he needed and got to work. The damage wasn't so bad, but he was annoyed to find the fifth gear cog was missing. That was something he'd have to bribe the lift attendant to get for him, and it could take a couple of days. This particular velocycle, by far his fastest, was the one he needed to train on. He flung down his tools, the double-page spread of a sky whale's digestive system winking at him from his desk.

Jackson had no interest in his studies. He didn't want to take over the family business and he didn't care about airship fleets or sky whale hotels. Jackson's father and the head of the Willoughby family, Edwin Willoughby, had entrusted his younger brother, Hamilton, with the running of the whale until Jackson was old enough to take over. But the thought of even visiting the Willoughby Whale, soaring up there so high in the Upper Atmosphere, made Jackson feel queasy. He'd prefer to keep both his feet firmly on the ground, thank you very much!

The only thing he was interested in was velocycles – racing velocycles, fixing velocycles, reading about velocycles, watching the Ravenport Racers racing velocycles, and dreaming about becoming a velocycle champion. He sneaked off to practise any time he could – and he was quick too. His race times were just as good as Franklyn Beaumont's had been at his age. The Racers try-outs were only two weeks away and those with the fastest times would be invited to join the team! The first step was to actually pass the time trials and get into their training camp. Once he had signed the team contract, he hoped there would be little his parents could do about it.

His favourite photo of the Ravenport Racers was pinned above his desk. It was taken the day they won the Championship, arms wrapped around each other's necks, beaming smiles, and Franklyn Beaumont at the centre of it all – head-ruffled, back-slapped, surrounded by love and respect.

This was what Jackson wanted more than anything and no one – not even Mrs Hogwood – was going to get in his way.

CHAPTER 3

At the end of every day, workers from Ravenport's shops, factories and scrapyards crammed themselves into the creaking service lift and today was no exception. Zeina squashed herself into a corner, desperately attempting to avoid the sweaty armpit of a large overalled woman. As the steel box clanked up the first few floors, Zeina watched the grey streets with their ant-like people and toy-like automobiles disappear into the thickening smog.

The people inside shared the exhausting job of turning the crank. It got easier floor by floor, as the factory workers, bank clerks, shop workers, maids and cooks disembarked.

An apprentice lawkeeper got out on floor twenty-one, followed by two airship stewards on floor twenty-five, leaving Zeina to take on the back-breaking work of raising the lift all alone.

As the lift approached floor twenty-eight, the little bulb above the door started to buzz and glow. When the lift stopped,

Zeina was relieved to see Shrapnel in his work overalls and goggles, grinning at her through the shutters.

"Ello, Zee! Move over then.' He screeched open the shutters and took over the lift handle. Zeina gratefully sank on to the bench, rubbing her throbbing arms. Shrapnel turned twelve last year, meaning he had already started his apprenticeship to become an engine-room worker. As his father had done before him, he spent long hours hauling and shovelling ore into the furnaces that powered the airships of the Willoughby fleet. In the last year, his shoulders had grown broad and he made light work of raising the lift despite his short stature.

'All the way to the top, is it, m'lady?' he said, eyes twinkling as he tipped an imaginary cap.

Zeina, still panting too hard to talk, stuck out her tongue.

Instead of living on one of these floors, Zeina's father, an engineer for the Willoughby family, had chosen to bring up his daughter in the tiny rooms adjoining his workshop on the airship platform. Despite the cramped conditions and the noise from hovering airships, not to mention the long, tiring journey in the service lift, Zeina wouldn't have chosen to live anywhere else. She could watch airships land and take off and listen to the aviators tell tales of their adventures in the Upper Atmosphere. She could ask junior air staff endless questions about sky whales. From her bedroom's tiny porthole window, she could look up into the clear sky above, sometimes even

16

spotting the shadow of a sky whale sailing high above her in the Upper Atmosphere. She could sit on her bed and watch and dream of what it would be like to see one in real life.

'Well then?' she asked Shrapnel, as soon as she had recovered. 'Has she arrived?'

'Who?' Shrapnel replied innocently.

'Shrapnel!'

'Oh . . . you mean a certain famous explorer of the four continents?'

'The greatest of all time!'

'An airship captain, style icon, pioneer of the Western Continent, discoverer of the Northern Ice Caves and, most importantly, personal hero of yours?' His eyes twinkled with mischief.

'*Shrapnel!*'

He laughed as she squared up to him. 'Yes, she's arrived. The legendary Miss Steele was spotted by yours truly boarding the Willoughby Whale yesterday evening. The *Raven*'s been docked there a couple of days, by all accounts. When I saw her, she was done up all glamorous-looking. Off to a party or something, I'd imagine.'

Zeina was both impressed and horribly jealous – she would do anything to see Vivianne Steele in real life.

'Maybe she'll come down for that big party the Willoughbys are having,' she said hopefully.

17

'Come down here? I wouldn't think so!' Shrapnel scoffed. 'She's only ever on this continent for a week or so before she goes off again. She's not going to waste any time in stinking Ravenport.'

'No, s'pose not.' Zeina tried to sound like she didn't care half as much as she did.

'Hey, there has been another raid though.' Shrapnel's eyebrows raised with excitement.

'Really?!'

'Yep. Last week. On the Bellafleur Whale – Smog Rats came out of nowhere! Their ship was completely silent and ridiculously fast. It was the same as last time; no one heard a thing. They stole everything – money, jewellery, gold – and then the whale bolted! The stewards only just managed to get everyone off and on to life-ships in time! Everyone up there is all worked up about it; there's lawkeepers all over the place.'

Zeina shuddered. The thought of lawkeepers made her feel just as uneasy as the pirates did. Lawkeepers were supposed to protect everyone, Aboves and Belows alike, but it often seemed that only ever the latter were arrested.

'The passengers must have been terrified.'

Shrapnel laughed. 'Terrified of giving up their jewels, maybe!'

'What about whoever designed the Smog Rat airship? Are the lawkeepers any closer to catching them?'

'Nah! They won't find them – could be anywhere on the four continents!'

'Your job is so exciting, Shrap,' said Zeina wistfully. 'Airships, sky whales, the Upper Atmosphere – that's what I want! Not to be stuck down here all the time. Dad won't even consider it though.'

'There's only so far shovelling ore can get you, Zee. I spend most of my time in a sweaty engine room. You'll make a great apprentice engineer and then you can get a job on an airship a few years down the line.'

Zeina wasn't sure she could wait years.

By now they had reached the airship platform. The shutters opened and in drifted the cool early-evening air along with the familiar smell of fuel. Zeina's father was deep in conversation with an aviator next to the rear propeller of an airship. He towered over the man, as he did most people. His shaggy hair was topped with an array of goggles and magnifiers, and his long leather apron, filled with tools and airship parts, hung almost to the floor. His fingers pulled absent-mindedly at his bristly beard, as they always did when he was thinking hard about something.

'Zeina!' he said, clasping her in a hug the moment he saw her. She breathed the scent of leather and airship grease and instantly felt at home. 'Where have you *been*?' he demanded sternly, giving her bulging backpack a prod. 'The platform's been crazy and you were supposed to be helping me out with all the comings and goings for this party.'

'I'm sorry, Dad.' Zeina gulped guiltily. 'I just lost track of time.'

For most of the year, Zeina attended Ravenport Industrial School for Belows, a rusted warehouse on the outskirts of town. There they learned 'basic skills', which included reading instructions, machine maintenance and airship stewardship, for ten hours a day, six days a week, eleven months of the year. Every August, however, when the smog was too toxic to attend school, Below children were free to do as they pleased for once, and, as always, Zeina was desperate to make the most of it.

'There'll be no swanning off on treasure hunts once your apprenticeship starts in a few months,' her father added, frowning. There had been a lot of this talk lately, "*Once you turn twelve*" *THIS* and "*When you start your apprenticeship*" *THAT*. Zeina had at one time been looking forward to starting work with her dad, maintaining the Willoughby airships – she couldn't wait to leave that stuffy school – but as it grew closer, the idea was becoming just as stifling.

'Aren't you going to be late for work, Shrap?' her father grumbled, seeing Shrapnel loitering behind the propeller and gossiping with one of the stewards. 'Off with you to the engine room before I report you!'

'Yes, sir! See ya, Zee!' He grabbed Zeina in a hug and saluted her dad before running off to join the air team for departure.

'I have a surprise. Something arrived for you this afternoon, although I'm not sure whether you deserve it now.' Her dad winked.

Zeina was ecstatic. She rarely got gifts and she never had anything delivered to her personally. Secretly, she hoped it might be something from the Vivianne Steele Fan Club. She had seen an advert in the paper a few weeks ago and had written to them explaining why, despite not having the money for the membership fee, she still deserved the welcome badge, poster and signed autograph of Miss Steele.

'Oh, please, Dad! I really am sorry. I promise that tomorrow I'll help you all day.'

Her father pulled out a golden envelope from the pocket of his apron. Zeina turned it over in her hands. The back was sealed with a shining W in melted wax and on the front, in silver swirling letters, was written 'Miss Zeina Starborn'.

'Oh!' Zeina couldn't help but show her disappointment – it didn't look like it was from the fan club. 'What is it?'

'Why don't you open it and see? I've already opened mine.'

Carefully, Zeina broke the wax and unfolded an invitation in matching silver and gold script.

Miss Zeina Starborn

YOU ARE CORDIALLY INVITED TO ATTEND THE ANNUAL

GRAND BIRTHDAY BAZAAR

CELEBRATING THE 12TH BIRTHDAY OF

Master Jackson Willoughby

SATURDAY AT 2 P.M.

FLOOR 45, WILLOUGHBY TOWERS

ꙮ DRESS CODE FOR THIS YEAR IS FANCY DRESS ꙮ

Written underneath in neat black pen was this addition:

Every year the Willoughbys thank their loyal employees by entering their children in a draw to attend the Grand Birthday Bazaar.

We are pleased to report that you have been selected!

Please arrive promptly and dress appropriately or admission may be denied.

'Are we going?' Zeina was incredulous. The party was on her last Saturday of freedom.

'Of course,' said her dad. 'We would offend the Willoughbys if we didn't and, anyway, I thought you'd want to go.'

'Why? Jackson Willoughby doesn't even know who we are.'

'Of course he does! We've been repairing his family's airships since he was born. He's a nice boy, Zeina – a bit shy but always polite.' He looked around carefully and lowered his voice. 'Some exceptions have to be made for the fact that his parents have essentially abandoned him to that awful housekeeper.'

Zeina thought about telling her dad about bumping into Jackson but decided against it. She feared her father, who had worked all his life for the Above family, would be disappointed to find out that it was likely none of the Willoughbys even knew his name.

'There will be mountains of food, I'd imagine,' her dad continued. 'Cakes, pies, pastries – and you wouldn't have to wear a dress or anything. Thought you might enjoy making a costume? There's the annual birthday surprise too. Last year it was a real striped horse from the Southern Continent and the year before, a demonstration by a velocycle team.'

Zeina did love making things out of scrap and had already thought of Vivianne Steele for a potential outfit. She had collected some old cracked monocles today that would be perfect for turning into the explorer's famous monocular spyglass. Her mouth was beginning to water at the thought of all that food too.

'OK,' Zeina said. 'Maybe it wouldn't be all bad.'

'There's my Zeina.' Her dad sighed with relief. 'Now, down

to your room. You better unpack today's finds and then wash up for dinner. I'm not sitting across from you covered in slime again.'

Thinking she'd got off lightly, Zeina did not have to be asked twice. She flew through the hatch that led to her dad's workshop and then down the stairs to their rooms. A curtain was all that separated her nook of a bedroom from their kitchen. Most of the space was taken up by Zeina's bed, but there was a tiny desk on one side, which held a framed photograph of her with her parents. Her dad's arms were wrapped around her mum, who was laughing as a gummy baby Zeina bounced on her knee. Her mum had died when she was small and this, her only photograph of them all together, was Zeina's most treasured possession.

One corner of her bedroom was decorated with photographs of the Ravenport Racers and pictures of sky whales, some hand-drawn and others torn out of scavenged books. There was also a whole wall dedicated to posters and photographs of Vivianne Steele. Her favourite was one of Miss Steele stepping down from her legendary airship, the *Raven*, on to the back of a sky whale, while the first structures of a hotel were being built around her. Vivianne was wearing her furs, smiling into the camera, leaning down to clink glasses with the new owner, while an enormous sign displaying 'WELCOME TO THE SAPPHIRE-REGENCY' was being hung from a girder behind them.

Zeina had painted the rest of her bedroom walls to show the four continents. At the head of her bed was the East, where she had painted Ravenport with a giant Willoughby Towers at its centre and carefully labelled each of the five atmospheric layers – something all would-be explorers should know by heart.

On the ground was *Street Level*, with its factories and warehouses, followed by the grey clouds of the *Smog Layer*. Zeina had added to this layer repeatedly over the years, as the pollution in her city got worse. Her annotation showing the smog-line had been painted over and moved up many times. Above this was the light-blue *Lower Atmosphere*, illustrated with smiling Aboves zooming between towers in small airships. Tiny figures of her and her dad had been added to the top of Willoughby Towers, waving off a large Upper Atmosphere airship as it ascended through the white puffs of the *Cloud Layer*. The dark-blue *Upper Atmosphere* extended up on to her ceiling and was covered with Zeina's imaginings of what it might be like up there – magnificent sky whale hotels, airships of every variety. A group of wild sky whales soared above her pillow.

On the opposite wall were paintings of the other three continents. The Northern Continent, white with snow, had Ice Bears and caves piled with treasures. The sandy

Southern Continent was covered with pictures of exotic animals. The Western Continent showed its tall mountains and trees. Zeina had tried to draw a picture of a Kotarth, the cat-like people who lived in the wild, dense forests. She had no idea how accurate it was, for she had never seen one in real life.

Zeina dug around in her bag, placing each of her finds on her desk. At the very bottom of her backpack she found a golden cog, far too shiny to be one she found at the dump. It must have fallen off Jackson's velocycle when they crashed into one another. She toyed with the idea of getting it back to him.

He probably won't even miss it, she thought. *I bet he's got a whole roomful at home.*

Incidentally, it was the perfect size – just what she was looking for to finish off her project.

In a box beneath her bed, covered in a sheet, lay her masterpiece. She ran her fingers over it lovingly, feeling the cool, hard metal. She unfolded the golden tube, hinged in the middle. At one end were two wooden airship propellers and the gears and pedals from a velocycle. It was to these she secured the golden cog and began to turn. The pedals now glided smoothly, just as she had anticipated. Finally, she pulled and folded the last of the parts and as everything clicked into place, she beamed. It was definitely going to work!

If she didn't feel guilty for the stolen cog, she certainly

did for the very last part she attached. It was one she had found hidden right at the back of her dad's desk drawer. Recently, her dad had been working harder and later than ever. She'd guessed the Willoughbys had him working on a new airship model – something that they didn't want the other Above families to know about. And when she found the plans and this part, she knew she was right.

It looked a little bit like a gas-lamp canister with a propeller attached to one side. She bolted it under the saddle and hopped on. Holding the handles and turning one of the gears, she started to pedal. To her immense joy, it jumped a little into the air, hovering a few centimetres off the ground. After a silent screech of victory, she tentatively angled the handlebars upwards and pedalled steadily. WHOOSH! Up it lurched, with such speed that she walloped her head on the ceiling and fell to the floor with an almighty clatter.

'Zeina? What was that? Are you OK?' Her father's voice drifted in through her window.

'Yes, I'm fine, Dad. Don't come in! I just . . . fell over. I'm getting changed. I'll be out in a minute!'

Despite the large, egg-shaped bump developing on her forehead, Zeina grinned – her "aerocycle" worked!

CHAPTER 4

A hammering on his door, followed by the high sing-song voice of Mrs Hogwood, assaulted Jackson's ears. 'Master Jackson, your guests are here!'

'Yes, Mrs Hogwood.'

Jackson regarded himself in the mirror. He looked ridiculous. Franklyn Beaumont had been his first choice for a costume but Mrs Hogwood would have none of it. Somehow the suggestion of his grandfather, Lord Clement Oswald Willoughby (Founder of the Willoughby Whale, the world's very first sky whale hotel), came up, and before he knew it there he was in an ancient frilled shirt, a floral brocade waistcoat, long striped trousers and an enormous top hat.

With his own bright copper hair and a matching copper-coloured curled moustache stuck to his face, he did indeed look just like the many portraits of Clement that were hung around the apartment.

Jackson sighed and opened his bedroom door.

Mrs Hogwood had gone all out on the decorations. The grand sitting room glittered with golden banners emblazoned with "Happy 12th Birthday, Jackson!". There were streamers, paper lanterns and towers of balloons, all in the Willoughby colours of navy and gold. Long tables in the dining room were laden with platters of meats, cheeses, cakes, eclairs, jellies and pastries. Smartly dressed servers hovered with trays of sparkling drinks and a band played their instruments gently over the chatter of the first guests. A mountain of brightly coloured presents towered next to the buffet.

Mrs Hogwood positioned Jackson in the entrance hall to greet the arriving guests. Some of the adults were in uniform – captains, admirals or commanders with gleaming medals pinned to their chests; others wore their very best clothes – vibrant suits and top hats or luxurious skirts with feathered caps. The children were all in costume – there were famous innovators, explorers and velocyclists, as well as a menagerie of creatures from the four continents, including an Ice Bear and a Kotarth queen. The boy dressed as an Ice Bear wore a big white fur coat, leather armour and false pointed teeth, and a younger-looking girl, dressed as the Kotarth queen, wore a silver crown around a pair of stick-on tufted ears, with a black nose and drawn-on whiskers. Jackson's hand was shaken vigorously by every guest.

Only one person did not seem impressed and that was a

girl about his age, dressed in an oversized aviator-style jacket and airship goggles, a red scarf holding her dark curls away from her face. By the homemade monocular spyglass that clanked at her belt, Jackson judged that she was supposed to be a famous explorer of some kind – Celia Brownsmith or Vivianne Steele, maybe. While her father greeted Jackson and thanked him warmly, she surveyed the room – chest puffed out and her nose, peppered with chestnut freckles, lifted proudly. Her amber eyes felt familiar to Jackson, and yet he could not place where he had seen them before.

After a nudge from her father, she turned to Jackson and bowed low. 'Happy birthday, Master Jackson!' she said with a flourish, an unmistakeable shadow of a smirk on her face. This irritated Jackson. No one was forcing her to be there – unlike him! And at least she could go straight to the buffet, the smell of which was making his insides ache with longing.

The line dragged on and on. Jackson's feet hurt and he was desperate to rip off the now impossibly itchy moustache. It seemed that every Above in the Eastern Continent had been invited. The only people he didn't see at all were his parents. Deep down he had known they wouldn't come home from their holiday just for his birthday, but it still made his chest tighten, like a tiny shard of ice to his heart.

After what seemed like hours, the queue of grinning,

bowing, curtsying guests finally dispersed. While Mrs Hogwood was distracted, Jackson escaped, ducking behind one of the tall decorated pot plants.

'Ow!'

He had stepped on something, no – *someone*. Someone crouching behind the same pot plant, and who had given his leg a sharp kick. The someone grabbed him roughly, pulled him down and clamped a hand across his mouth. It was the same red-scarfed, rude girl from the line. With her other hand she placed a finger to her lips, fixing him with a fiery glare before drawing one finger across her throat. This might have looked more menacing were it not for a smudge of jam around one side of her mouth.

'Ssssh!' she hissed.

It was only then Jackson realised that this was actually the third time in a week that this girl had been rude to him for no apparent reason. He hadn't recognised her at first, minus the slime, but now, with that furious frown, he knew it was the same girl who had bumped into him with his velocycle.

'It's you! What are you doing here?' he whispered back, once his mouth was released.

'Oh, of course. What would *I* be doing here? A commoner like me at your party.' Her voice grew louder and louder.

'Ssssh! No, I meant what are you doing *here*, behind the plant?'

'Hiding from your stupid housekeeper, of course,' she replied. 'She's already shouted at me three times.'

'I'm hiding from Hogwood too, actually,' Jackson admitted.

'Why are you hiding?' the girl demanded, incredulous. 'Surely you can order her to do whatever you like. These people are all your guests.'

Jackson laughed. 'No one orders Mrs Hogwood to do anything. I don't even know most of the guests. Most are business associates of my mum and dad's, people who come with gifts for me to try and impress them.'

'Poor you, having to accept all those large, expensive gifts.'

Suddenly the chatter of guests was silenced by the clinking of glass. The band stopped playing and the attention of everyone, including the girl's, was captured by a tall man dressed in a particularly loud green suit. Jackson sighed heavily.

'Attention, all! Your attention, please!' the man boomed. In one hand he held a sparkling glass of champagne and in the other a gold pocket watch, which he placed carefully back inside the pocket of his red-patterned waistcoat. On his head was a matching top hat adorned with a large ruby brooch and a luxurious green peacock feather. He twirled his magnificent mahogany moustache and smiled welcomingly, his dark eyes glinting, one of which was magnified behind an ornate gold monocle.

32

'Good afternoon to you all! To those who may not know who I am,' he chortled, 'my name is Hamilton Willoughby, Lord Willoughby's younger, and some would say more handsome, brother! Captain of the Willoughby Whale and uncle to the darling birthday boy! Where is he? Where is the special boy?'

'Go on then!' the girl hissed.

'No, wait!' Jackson hissed back, but it was too late. She barged him roughly from his hiding place and, hat askew and moustache half off, straight into the crowd.

'Oh, there you are, my dear boy!' Hamilton pointed to Jackson, making every eye turn to him. His heart fell to his stomach. Other than heights, the only thing Jackson feared was being the centre of attention.

'Come now, Jackson.' Hamilton beckoned. 'It's not like us Willoughbys to be shy!' He chortled again. Laughter rippled from the crowd as Jackson, pink-cheeked, made his way towards the front. Jackson had only met his uncle a handful of times and had disliked him more each time. The thought of moving to the Willoughby Whale to start his apprenticeship with him made Jackson feel sick.

'Now, everyone, please join me . . . Happy birthday to you, happy birthday to you . . .'

The whole room sang to Jackson, as his cheeks turned from pink to crimson. Four staff brought out a giant cake in the shape of the Willoughby emblem – an enormous golden W. There were impressed whispers from the crowd, followed by a cheer as Jackson blew out twelve candles.

'There you go, my dearest chap!' Hamilton smacked Jackson on the back, making him cough. 'May your year be filled with joy! And what a year it is going to be for you!' His tone became serious and his voice even more dramatic. 'Why, this is just the start of Jackson's journey to prepare himself for the great honour that lies before him. As the Willoughby heir, he will one day take over from my dearest brother, Edwin, to become Head of the Willoughby Company, responsible for our fleet of airships and, indeed, the Willoughby Whale, the largest and most luxurious whale hotel in any of the four continents!'

There was a cheer from the room as Jackson's stomach sank to the floor. Hamilton dramatically dabbed at his eyes with a spotted handkerchief. 'It has been such an honour to aid my dearest brother all these years and I only hope, dearest Jackson, that one day my beloved Herbert can help you in the same way.'

The room let out a loud 'Awww' as Hamilton grabbed Jackson under one arm and a pale lad with a moody glower on his face with the other. Cousin Herbert was dressed in a suit as awful as his father's. Despite being well above the smog-line, he was also wearing an enormous respirator mask, which only made his outfit look more ridiculous.

'And now for this year's Grand Surprise!' Hamilton's tone switched to one of jubilation. 'Edwin and I thought that, considering the year ahead of you, my boy, it would be fitting for you and one of your young guests here today to start the year with the trip of a lifetime!' He paused to enjoy the cheers from the crowd, his eye twinkling behind his monocle. 'Yes, my dear boy, you will accompany me and Herbert back to the Willoughby Whale, where you will stay in the most luxurious rooms on board and be the guests of honour at our Summer Ball, where you will meet the one and only, and most splendid personal friend of mine, Miss Vivianne Steele!'

Jackson reeled. He could not think of anything he would like to do less. So far he had managed to worm his way out of visiting Hamilton and Herbert on the Willoughby Whale. He knew the day would come when he could avoid it no longer but had always hoped it would be at least after he passed his exams. But the other guests were very impressed – gasping and chattering as Hamilton let out another satisfied chuckle. Even the rude girl appeared from behind her plant pot, wiping the jam from her cheek, her eyes wide with disbelief.

'Ha ha! Yes, my darling guests, Miss Steele would like nothing more than to meet my beloved nephew and future head of the Willoughbys. What an honour, my boy!'

Jackson attempted to shrink away, but Hamilton enveloped him in an enormous hug.

Jackson wanted the ground to swallow him whole but managed to whisper, 'Thank you very much,' in between more back-slapping. 'One thing, Uncle . . . When will I return exactly? It's just I've got my exams soon.' He was, of course, thinking of the time trials rather than his exams. He only had ten days left to train.

'Exams? Yuck! Who needs those? Certainly not you, my dear boy!' He lowered his voice so that only Jackson could hear. 'Never passed any of mine and got on just fine. We shall leave this very evening and you will be back within the week, so no need to fear Mrs Hogwood!'

Jackson breathed an inward sigh of relief. Despite the cold dread he felt at the thought of the airship flight, staying so high in the Upper Atmosphere, at least he'd be back in time for the trials.

'And now to select the lucky guest who will accompany you!' Hamilton boomed. Parents began to push their daughters and sons forward; children waved their hands excitedly in the air.

'Now, it would not be fair to ask my poor nephew to choose who will accompany him on this amazing trip, so we have collected the invitations of all children here today, placed them in this box and my dearest Herbert will randomly select a winner.'

Herbert stepped forward sulkily, holding a large wooden box.

'Drum roll, please!'

The whole crowd drummed and stamped, everyone apart from the rude girl, who was so still she appeared to not even be breathing. Herbert yawned behind his respirator, drawing out a gold invitation and handing it to his father.

'We are honoured to announce the winner ... Zeina Starborn!'

There was a shocked gasp from the room. Jackson heard disgruntled murmurs of, 'What did he say?', 'Who?', 'Never even heard of the Starborns!' Jackson squinted into the crowd, also unfamiliar with the name.

There was a sudden movement – the rude girl's father, the bearded man who had shaken Jackson's hand earlier. He moved quickly to her side, placing a protective hand upon her shoulder. She seemed completely dazed, frozen to the spot. Not her! Anyone but her! Mrs Hogwood glared at the girl, thunderous with anger. But it was too late. Hamilton was already cupping his hand above his eyes, bellowing into the crowd, 'Come up here, you lucky girl!'

The girl looked up at her father, who nodded reluctantly and released her. As she pushed her way through the shocked throng, a massive grin blooming on her face, his expression remained unreadable under his bushy moustache and beard.

'There you are!' Hamilton exclaimed. 'Come now, hurry up! Oh, how very apt, a little Vivianne Steele! Obviously this was meant to be!' Hamilton chortled, grabbing Jackson and Zeina to him closely. 'Now, let's have another cheer for the birthday boy and the very lucky Miss Starborn! Hip hip . . .'

CHAPTER 5

'**Y**ou're *not going*.'

Zeina had known this was coming. She'd known as soon as she saw her dad's face, grey and grave, as Hamilton embraced her and she was photographed by the press. The fact she knew it was coming didn't make it any less painful.

'You're joking? Dad!'

Her father wouldn't look at her. Instead he busied himself with the dishes left in the sink from breakfast.

'Zeina, it's impossible. That's all there is to it.'

'But why?' Whenever she broached the subject of airship travel, it was the same – her dad would close up like a clam. She had tried on many occasions to ask about going to work with Shrapnel for a day or two, just to see if she'd like it before her apprenticeship started, but his response was always the same: no way and no discussion.

'You've got too much to do here, Zeina.'

'You could manage without me for a few days, you know you could! If I can't go, I at least deserve to know the real reason why.'

He didn't answer, staring resolutely at the porridge pan he was scrubbing.

'You can't stop me,' she spat, suddenly furious, whirling away from him to charge helter-skelter into her bedroom.

Her dad appeared in the doorway. 'Zeina, please be reasonable. You are still so young and this trip is too dangerous for you right now. There are things you don't understand about this world, Zeina—'

'I understand plenty!' she snapped, flinging clothes, books and her favourite photograph of Vivianne Steele into her backpack. 'This has got nothing to do with the trip – this is about you not wanting to be alone. Since Mum died, I'm all you've got and you're scared that once I go and see how amazing it is up there, I won't ever want to come back.'

Zeina felt immediately guilty seeing the hurt expression on her dad's face, but refused to look away.

'I'm not saying that some of that isn't true, Zeina,' he replied, wide eyes haunted by grief. 'But it's my job . . .' He gulped, his voice suddenly high and squeaky, and Zeina knew he was holding back tears. 'Since your Mum . . . My job alone . . . to keep you safe. It's just too dangerous.'

Zeina wavered but knew she had to carry on. 'But it's not

too dangerous for Jackson Willoughby?' she asked more gently.

'It's different for people like him, Zeina,' he sniffed, eyes brimming with tears. 'You must stay here in Ravenport where I can keep an eye on you.'

'You can't keep me here for ever, Dad.'

'I know. But while I can, I will.' He blinked, and a solitary tear trickled down his face and into his beard. She knew she couldn't leave him; she shouldn't have brought up Mum.

'Fine.' She turned away from him, her anger competing with the ache she felt at seeing her dad cry.

'I need to go and help get the airship off. It's probably best if you stay here and avoid—'

'Fine, Dad. Just go.'

Zeina curled up in a ball on her bed. She refused to cry, despite the unfairness of it all. The voices of the aircrew arriving for their shifts floated down through the half-open window in her ceiling. Despite herself, she reached up to open the porthole fully and listen to the noises of the airship getting ready to leave, taking her dream away with it. She heard the roll of the gangway being pushed up to the deck, the stewards heaving luggage into the hold, the engines starting up, pistons clanking gently and then the 'ding-ding' of the automatic lift as the Above passengers drifted out of the party and up to the platform to board.

An unmistakeably haughty 'Hurry up!' told her that Mrs Hogwood had arrived with Jackson. There was a flurry of steps and then her dad's voice rose above the rest.

'I'm sorry, Mrs Hogwood, Zeina isn't feeling well this evening and won't be able to come on the trip after all. I've had to put her to bed. Please accept our apologies, Master Jackson.'

Mrs Hogwood's tone did nothing to hide how ecstatic she was. 'Oh well, these things can't be helped!'

'Zeina and I hope you have a really lovely trip, Jackson,' her dad added. 'I know that Mr Hamilton likes to remain in his cabin for take-off so I have written a letter explaining everything. Will you give it to him on Zeina's behalf, Jackson?'

'Of course, Mr Starborn.'

'It's for the best, Jackson,' Hogwood said brightly. 'You can spend more time on your studies and poor Miss Starborn would have felt most out of place, I'm sure.'

'That may be.' Her father's voice was low and clipped. 'Enjoy your trip, Jackson.'

White-hot fury coursed back into Zeina. How dare they – all of them – decide what was best for her? What her place in this world should be? Mrs Hogwood. Her dad. Even Jackson Willoughby. The obvious relief she heard in his voice when he had found out she was no longer accompanying him hurt Zeina more than any of Mrs Hogwood's snide remarks. More so even than her father telling Jackson to enjoy his trip. How could he wish that for Jackson but not her?

This was *her* dream trip, *her* once-in-a-lifetime opportunity and nothing and nobody, not Mrs Hogwood or her dad or Jackson Willoughby, was going to stop her. An idea was beginning to form in her head. She just had to get to Jackson before he gave that letter to Hamilton!

The grind of the gangway being pulled back, the whirling propellers and the acrid smell of burning ore told her that she had to hurry. She grabbed some scrap paper from her desk, gulping down a gurgle of guilt as she scrawled her message.

Dad,
I'm sorry but I have to go. I love you.
Please don't worry. I'll be careful.
See you in a few days.
Z xxx

A lump in her throat formed as she placed it on her pillow for him to find. She pushed away the thought of his kind eyes wide with hurt as he read that note. She grabbed her aerocycle from its hiding place, unfolded it, slung on her backpack, hopped up to her bed and positioned herself above the saddle. Making sure the circular window in her ceiling was open as much as possible, she took a deep breath – timing was key.

The whirring of the airship's engines reached a crescendo as it hovered above the platform surface. It was now or never.

'Work, please work,' she said out loud, clicking the gears and kicking off, her feet reaching desperately for the pedals. For a moment, she felt she'd simply fall to the floor. But then there was a lurch in the pit of her stomach as the aerocycle leapt into the air. She did her best to contain a squeal of excitement, pedalling steadily so that just her head peeped out of the window. The hull of departing airships always came low over her window as they turned away from Ravenport. She had grown used to the sudden darkness engulfing her room and would count the seconds until the sunlight returned.

The darkness came. 'One, two, three, four, five,' she counted slowly, and then began pedalling, launching vertically through the open window, her head bent low over the handlebars so that her backpack would fit.

She was out! Flying alongside the hull of the rotating airship, she was obscured from the rest of the platform and – most importantly – her dad. Dodging the giant propellers, she sped forwards, grabbing on to a small sliding door in the hull and flinging herself, her backpack and the aerocycle safely into the luggage hold. She laughed with relief. She'd made it!

As they rose, the towers of Ravenport were silhouetted against the red-orange glow of the setting sun and any regrets she might have had were lost to the wind.

CHAPTER 6

Jackson was about four years old when his parents took him up into the Upper Atmosphere to see the Willoughby Whale for the very first time. He could remember feeling excited, pleased that his parents were actually taking him with them for once. He also remembered how quickly that excitement had turned to terror.

Once in the air, the sight of all that sky, stretching out around and underneath the airship, terrified him. He cried and wouldn't move from behind his mother's skirt and his dad grew so angry that he told the captain to turn around. They never made it to the whale and his dad never took him out on his airship again.

Standing on the deck of Hamilton's airship, the *Sparrowhawk*, all those feelings came flooding back. Jackson's heart pounded as if it was trying to escape from his chest and his stomach swam with sickness and shame. He looked down at his arms, pale and goose-pimpled, and his hands, white-knuckled, tightly gripping the banister of the decking.

The *Sparrowhawk* rose, slowly at first, then steadily, the pistons becoming louder and louder. The propellers, once free from the platform surface, began to whirl as the airship turned and tilted up into the Lower Atmosphere.

The towers of Ravenport seemed to loom away and then towards him menacingly. Rocking backwards and forwards, he screwed his eyes shut, breathing steadily in and out. 'It'll be better soon,' he whispered to himself. 'Once we're through the cloud layer. Once you can't see Ravenport any more.'

A nearby CRASH drew him from his thoughts. The few passengers who had decided to stay out on deck were crowded round something on the floor.

'I'm fine. Stop fussing. I'm fine!'

Distracted from his fear, Jackson pushed his way to the front of the crowd. There lay Zeina in a crumpled heap, long limbs twisted around something that looked strangely like a velocycle.

'Zeina?'

'She flew up from the luggage hold!' one man shouted. 'She flew on that velocycle!' He was pointing at the velocycle-like thing, which Jackson could now see had a pair of ancient airship propellers attached where the wheels would usually be.

'Don't be ridiculous,' Zeina said, dusting herself off. 'This is clearly not a velocycle. It's called an aerocycle.'

'Whatever it is, you could have killed my wife!' the man continued, a terrified woman clutched to his side.

'Well, it's not my fault she just stood there gawping like an idiot,' Zeina replied, calmly folding parts of the strange machine inward, until it was small enough to place inside her backpack.

The man's face was growing redder and redder. Jackson grabbed Zeina by the arm and pulled her away before she could make the situation even worse.

'What are you doing here?'

'I was invited! You were there. I won the trip fair and square, and so here I am!'

'But your father said you were sick. He gave me this to give to—'

She snatched the letter out of his hand and tore it in two, throwing the pieces overboard with a grin.

'As you can see, I'm fine. If anyone's sick, it's you. You look positively green!'

Standing by the railings again, he did indeed feel like he was about to throw up. The platform of Willoughby Towers was too small to see now. Hundreds of tower tops making up the Above part of Ravenport stretched out beneath them. Higher and higher they flew, until the greying landscape surrounding Ravenport could be seen through shifting smog. Abandoned parks, decaying suburbs and a crumbling quarry, its drills and machinery rusted into strange sculptures in the evening light. The river sludged through the northern part of the city, around scrapyards and landfill and, beyond that, the scorched patchwork of once-green fields. To the east, Jackson spotted a clearing; the industrial fans of the Ravenport Racers stadium whirred, signalling that they must be practising.

He closed his eyes again, wishing he was down there on his velocycle. When he opened them again Zeina was watching him curiously.

'You're not scared of flying, are you?' Her nose crinkled in disbelief.

'No, of course not! I've been up here dozens of times,' he lied unconvincingly.

'You *are* scared! *But* you're going to be in charge of your own fleet of airships one day.'

'I'm *not* afraid! I've just seen it before, that's all.'

Zeina raised an eyebrow. Jackson focused hard on the wooden floorboards of the deck, but they became all blurry. Unable to stand any longer, he slumped to the floor.

'I'll be all right once we're through the clouds,' he admitted. 'Once Ravenport isn't in view.'

Jackson didn't have to wait long; a minute later, the funnels, then the deck and the hull of the airship were

48

engulfed by the cloud layer. They could see nothing but white for a second and then the ship burst through into a vast, moon-lit navy, dotted with stars. Zeina, who had sat down next to Jackson, gazed up in awe.

'The Upper Atmosphere is beautiful, isn't it?'

Jackson agreed begrudgingly.

'It would be a shame if Hamilton found out that there had been a last-minute change of plan and I'm not supposed to be here after all,' she said tentatively. 'He might send me home. I'd miss all this.' She paused, an uneasy minute of silence, before continuing, 'I suppose your uncle doesn't know you're scared of heights?'

Jackson, unsure what she was getting at exactly, decided it was safest to simply say nothing at all.

'And I suppose your family don't know about your velocycle plan yet, either? That day we bumped into each other, you said you were practising for the time trials, but then at your party Hamilton seemed to think you'd be starting your job with the family business this year. And Mrs Hogwood was going on about you studying for your exams.'

'Wait a minute, are you blackmailing me?'

'No! It's just . . . withholding certain information in a way that would be mutually beneficial to us both.' She grinned. 'An agreement, a truce, a deal, if you will?' She held out her hand for him to shake.

49

Despite his annoyance, Jackson could see he had no choice but to agree. The thought of Zeina being sent home as soon as they reached the Willoughby Whale pleased him immensely, but he couldn't risk Hamilton finding out about the Ravenport Racers time trials. He sighed and reluctantly shook her hand.

CHAPTER 7

'Already getting along splendidly, I see!'

There was a familiar chortle from behind Zeina as Hamilton Willoughby appeared, wearing a travelling cloak of rich purple.

'Come now, Miss Starborn, away from the edge, if you please! Your father would never forgive us if we lost you overboard! Ho ha! Is that all the luggage you have, my dear?' he asked, pointing to her battered backpack. 'Here, give it to me and I'll get a steward to take it to your cabin.' He clicked his fingers, passing the bag to the steward who appeared instantly at his side. Herbert arrived in an identical purple cloak, his thin, pale lips curving into a smirk as he examined Zeina's outfit. She hadn't had time to change out of her Vivianne Steele costume.

'You'll forgive our absence at take-off, my dears. Herbert's chest is extremely sensitive to the conditions in Ravenport, isn't it, dearest?' Hamilton's baby voice as he said the word 'dearest', despite Herbert being at least ten, made Zeina feel quite sick.

'Yes, Father. How do you cope, Miss Starborn? You actually live on that awful platform! The fumes and dust must be quite unbearable! Oh, I simply can't wait for you to see the Whale for the first time!' His sickeningly sweet voice did nothing to hide the maliciousness in his eyes.

'It will be around oh-six-hundred hours by my calculations,' said Hamilton, taking his golden pocket watch from his waistcoat. 'They are cruising a few miles above us, towards the western border. Now, we must show Miss Starborn around! I hear you have never been on an airship at all, my dear? Imagine spending all that time covered in airship grease but never actually going on one!'

Hamilton's tour included the upper deck, reserved for VIPs, and the bridge, where they were introduced to the captain. They inspected the giant funnels and the magnificent clanking pistons. He showed them the engine room, where they took in the glowing furnaces and the grunting, shovelling crew, grey with dust and sweat. Zeina hoped she might see Shrapnel; she could just imagine his face if he saw her being shown round the ship like a guest of honour!

After the engine room, Hamilton showed them the lower deck, which he had turned into a Willoughby family gallery. There were portraits of Jackson's ancestors, exhibits celebrating the family's successes, a statue of Jackson's grandfather 'Founder of The First Sky Whale Hotel' and photographs of Willoughbys alongside other Aboves. One photo showed Jackson's father shaking hands with the Mayor of Ravenport; another was of Hamilton posing in a magnificent hat next to Franklyn Beaumont. Hamilton showed Zeina each in turn, talking at length, especially when the exhibit was about himself. Zeina noticed that Jackson stood for a long time looking gloomily at a photo of his parents in evening dress. The plaque underneath read:

Lord Edwin Willoughby and Lady Marjory Willoughby host a dinner every year aboard their famous airship, the *Golden Eagle,* to raise funds for their charity – The Willoughby Home for Orphaned, Aged, Troubled or Destitute Belows.

Zeina listened politely to Hamilton for as long as she could but soon her eye was caught by a particularly gruesome picture. It was of a wild sky whale – open-mouthed, pointed teeth glinting in jagged rows – attacking an antique airship, and Hamilton was too deep in conversation with himself to notice her sneaking away. Zeina had always been fascinated by sky whales, but as a Below, such things were not covered in her education. What she knew about them she had gleaned from snippets of information from aircrew staff, and newspapers and books she found at the scrapyard.

The grisly photo in question was part of a newspaper article. From the make and model of the airship, Zeina could tell it was many years old – probably early Second or even First Age. The headline read **"HUNDREDS FEARED DEAD IN FOURTH SKY WHALE ATTACK THIS YEAR"**. Zeina glanced at Hamilton, who, oblivious to her absence, was still telling nobody in particular about how much Franklyn Beaumont had admired his hat. She turned back to the newspaper's plaque.

THE THREE AGES OF THE GREAT SKY WHALE

The Age of Fear

Little is known about the Great Sky Whale (*Balaenagigas celestia*), discovered by Sir Bartholomew on one of his first expeditions into the Upper Atmosphere over 150 years ago. At approximately 900 metres in length, they were a fearsome foe of early explorers. As travel in the Upper Atmosphere became more common, frequent clashes between airships and sky whales resulted in numerous tragedies. The ferociousness of wild sky whales became legendary and early airship crews lived in constant fear of attack.

(See exhibit 101 – newspaper article *The Daily Herald.*)

Despite the fear etched into the faces of the ancient airship crew, Zeina couldn't help but wish she had been there to see it in real life. To her the sky whale was magnificent rather than terrifying. She continued to a second plaque, positioned below.

The Age of Conquest

Airships soon became more advanced and developed weapons to defend themselves against sky whale attacks.
(See exhibit 102 – this steam-driven harpoon from the *Silver Sparrow* was famous for defending its crew from three separate whale attacks.)
Thus began the Second Age of the Great Sky Whale. The need for both safe travel within the Upper Atmosphere and airship fuel meant that brave whaler crews were sent to track and hunt the most aggressive sky whales. Once caught, their blubber was processed to make valuable fuel and their thick skins could be turned into various products.
(See exhibit 103 – sky whale leather shoes.)
Humans at last were able to explore the four continents, safe in the knowledge they were not in danger.

To the right of the plaque was a long glass cabinet containing an impressive silver harpoon and a pair of children's shoes made of a thick grey leather. The great creases of grey skin across the tiny baby straps made Zeina feel rather odd. There was also a vintage advertising poster for the Willoughby Whale. A grinning cartoon whale carried a beaming man in a navy Willoughby uniform. The flourished gold letters underneath read:

THE GRAND OPENING OF
THE WILLOUGHBY WHALE
AN UPPER ATMOSPHERE EXPERIENCE LIKE NO OTHER!

There was a third plaque next to a photograph of a man who looked unmistakeably like an older Jackson Willoughby. He smiled proudly underneath an exuberant moustache.

The Age of Friendship

Unfortunately, decades of hunting meant that sky whale numbers decreased dramatically, and airships could no longer rely upon blubber for fuel. Sightings of sky whales in the Upper Atmosphere became rare, and decades went by when few humans encountered these vicious but magnificent beasts. It wasn't until Lord Clement Willoughby discovered and manufactured the Sky-whale Training And Navigating (STAN) System that they could return safely into our lives. Finally, sky whales could be tamed and used for transport. Since Lord Clement opened the first, most famous and most luxurious sky whale hotel, 'The Willoughby Whale', many other families have bought the STAN system and in this Third Age of the great sky whale, whales and humans are able to live and travel together in perfect harmony.

Jackson appeared by her side, staring moodily at the photograph.

'So your grandad, like, *invented* sky whale hotels?'

'Yes,' he said bitterly. 'He was obsessed with flying and sky whales. My father is too. He hates Ravenport, or anywhere on land, really.'

'And what is the STAN system?' Zeina had never even heard of it before – something else Belows didn't need to understand, she supposed.

'Grandad invented it but I don't really know how it works – it calms the whales down somehow. Stops them attacking humans. It's top secret. That way the other families have to pay us to have their own sky whale hotels.'

Zeina couldn't decide whether Jackson was keeping things from her on purpose or whether he was actually so dull that he hadn't bothered to find out about how his own grandad's revolutionary invention had changed the world. She vowed to ask Shrapnel what he knew about the STAN system as soon as she saw him next.

Underneath the last plaque was a crisp paper poster, tacked to the wall. The title read '**VIGILANCE WILL BE REWARDED**' and below were ten mugshots, showing several men and women, all scowling and vicious-looking.

BEWARE!

THE *NIGHTJAR* SMOG RATS ARE CURRENTLY OPERATING WITHIN THIS CONTINENT

ANY INFORMATION OR SIGHTINGS SHOULD BE REPORTED TO YOUR AIRSHIP (OR WHALE) LAWKEEPER-IN-CHIEF IMMEDIATELY.

REWARDS FOR INFORMATION THAT LEADS TO AN ARREST WILL BE SUBSTANTIAL.

IN THE EVENT OF AN ATTACK, PLEASE KEEP CALM AND FOLLOW THE INSTRUCTIONS OF STEWARDS.

STAY VIGILANT, STAY SAFE.

The Smog Rats were just one more thing – along with airship travel, the Upper Atmosphere and sky whales – that her dad simply refused to answer questions about. What she had learned was mainly from Shrapnel's gossip and from sneaky glimpses of newspapers when her dad wasn't looking. It all seemed terrifyingly exciting.

'Do you think there might be a Smog Rat attack while we're on board?' she asked Jackson, sounding almost hopeful.

Jackson shuddered. 'I hope not! They look horrible.

Definitely wouldn't want to bump into that one on a dark night.' He pointed at a picture of a woman with a ragged scar where her left eye should be.

Even if he was clueless about the STAN system, Zeina judged that, as an Above, Jackson might be a good source of information about the Smog Rats. She imagined them all sitting around and worrying about their jewels and riches, wondering where the next attack might be.

'So what do you know about the Smog Rats?' she asked, keeping her tone as polite and pleasant as she could manage.

'Not much,' replied Jackson. 'I know there used to be lots of Smog Rat raids in the olden days, attacking airstaff and stealing stuff, but then the lawmakers stopped unregistered airships from buying ore and they all sort of disappeared.'

'What about these lot?'

'First attack was last year. Out of nowhere came a new Smog Rat ship – the *Nightjar*. It raided the Ruby Oswald Hotel one night. Their ship is so silent that nobody heard it coming. They stole money and jewellery and caused so much damage to the STAN system that the whale got frightened and then bolted, up above the limit of the Upper Atmosphere – never to be seen again. Humans can't breathe up there, so it was lucky everyone was evacuated in time.'

'How many raids have there been since then?' She could do little to hide her excitement now.

'Five, I think, including that one last week on the Bellafleur.'

'Why haven't they been caught? It can't be that hard for all the lawkeepers across the continents to find *one* airship. Surely they have to get ore from somewhere?'

'My tutor says that they must have a secret ore mine in the Western Continent somewhere. Lawkeepers have searched for them, obviously, but it's too hard to find them in the smog layer.' His eyes twinkled rather smugly; the fact he was enjoying giving her all this information made it all the more irritating.

'Biggest mystery of all is who built and designed the ship itself. It's brand-new tech! "The Innovator" – that's who everyone is looking for, really. Until we have a ship as fast and as quiet as theirs, nobody stands a chance. Every whale has a guard or two onboard but there are far too many to send extra lawkeepers to every single one so—'

'Now, Jackson, what's all this whispering?'

Hamilton had stopped talking long enough to realise that neither of the children were still on his tour. He drew in a dramatic gasp when he saw they were in front of the Smog Rat poster and moved towards them, placing an unwelcome hand upon Zeina's shoulder.

'I do hope you're not telling stories to scare Miss Starborn. Wicked boy! Don't let Jackson here alarm you in any way, my dear.'

'Oh, he wasn't.' Zeina was rarely scared of anything. 'I was just wondering—'

'You don't need to be brave, my dear!' Hamilton interrupted, gripping both her shoulders and staring at her intensely through his monocle. 'You *must* be terrified! A young girl like you. But really, my dear, aboard the Willoughby Whale there is no cause for concern. For we are the largest and most magnificent whale hotel to have ever existed! In fact, the Senior Lawkeeper of Ravenport, a personal friend of mine, has sent us *five* extra lawkeepers. There really is no reason to be afraid.'

'Oh . . . thanks.'

The thought of the five extra lawkeepers worried Zeina far more than any Smog Rats.

CHAPTER 8

I t was still dark when Jackson was awoken by a brisk knocking upon his cabin door. Blurry-eyed, he made his way over and was confronted by a horrifying swathe of yellow.

One steward carried a long-tailed butterscotch jacket with matching checked trousers; the other a high-collared shirt, a canary cravat, a gold-buttoned waistcoat and a top hat made from fine caramel felt.

'Master Willoughby, this is a gift from Mr Hamilton. He asks that you wear it for our arrival this morning at the Willoughby Whale.'

'Oh, uh – thanks.' Jackson took the monstrous outfit and begrudgingly put it on while the stewards waited.

He was ushered up to the open-air terrace at the ship's bow, where a number of passengers were already gathered. A breakfast of exotic fruits, croissants, muffins, toast and waffles was being arranged on a large white-clothed table.

The sight of Zeina waiting there with Hamilton and Herbert forced Jackson to stifle a laugh. It wasn't just her ridiculous outfit – a butter-yellow dress of frilled lace, a lemon tailcoat jacket with enormous puffy sleeves, and sunshine velvet gloves embroidered with giant daisies – but her face. Never had he seen anyone look so angry. He pursed his lips, managing to suppress his snigger, but not before Zeina caught his eye and scowled at him from underneath her yellow-feathered fascinator.

'And don't we all look marvellous!' Hamilton boomed. 'You see how clever I am? I have dressed us in the Willoughby colours!' It was true; he and Herbert were wearing equally ridiculous outfits in different shades of navy. 'There will undoubtedly be press photographers waiting for us,' he winked, 'and we all must look our best!'

There was a flurry of excitement near the bow of the ship and Hamilton rudely pushed the children through the crowd.

'Out of the way, if you please!'

Jackson flushed, mumbling apologies as they made their way to the very front. The rising sun was changing the vast sky from a dark midnight to a bright cobalt; it loomed at Jackson, making him sway. He gripped the handrail as tightly as he could with his clammy hands and forced himself to open his eyes. He couldn't stand the thought of his uncle or

63

cousin noticing how terrified he was. In the very distance was a teeny grey smudge.

'Is that it?' Zeina's tone did little to hide her disappointment.

'Oh, how rude of us! Herbert, you must lend your spyglasses to Miss Starborn at once! It isn't every day you see your first real-life sky whale, now, is it?'

'Of course, Father. You must forgive my thoughtlessness, Miss Starborn. I do apologise,' Herbert simpered, handing her a handsome pair of chrome binoculars.

For once, Zeina was speechless, her eyes wide and mouth open slightly as she gazed through the eyepieces. After a minute or two of manipulating the little wheel on the top to zoom in and out, she handed the binoculars over to Jackson, a broad smile illuminating her face.

Jackson had spent many, many hours reading thick, boring, hard-backed books about sky whales; *A Natural History of Sky Whales*, *Essential Whale Management* and *A Concise History of Common Whale Law* were all required reading for any Above heir. However, to see one for the first time in real life gave Jackson an odd twisting sensation in the pit of his stomach.

Through the lenses, the rough texture of the great whale's hide leapt into view, scrapes and grooves magnified like deep scratches on the hull of an airship. He zoomed out a little. The whale was blueish-grey in colour with a mottled underbelly the colour of newly forged steel. White teeth protruded from an upturned mouth and its huge eye was dark and unblinking, a bottomless pool of inky water.

Jackson knew that the Willoughby Whale was the largest sky whale hotel in existence. Since his grandfather first captured it from the wild almost fifty years ago, it had quadrupled in size. Each great flipper was now the size of at least ten airship platforms and the whale itself easily the length of two Willoughby Towers stood one on top of the other. The body stretched out and tapered into a sweeping tail, curved flukes rising and sinking in a slow, graceful dance. Bolted around the great beast's middle were sheets of metal that had been hammered and welded into a harness. This was the base of the hotel – the first structure laid down after the STAN system was fitted – and it was on to this harness that all the other parts of the hotel had been built. Starting with the glass-domed observation deck near its head, towers, turrets and archways had been built, one on top of another, to form what looked like a magnificent city riding upon the beast's back. As the whale grew, the harness was adjusted and extended, making more and more room for extra buildings and attractions. Jackson spotted the parapet of the Grand Casino near the tail, the last addition to be erected before the whale had stopped growing. The harness appeared tight in places, the metal shell cutting deep grooves into the thick grey hide, and Jackson couldn't help but wonder if it was uncomfortable for the creature and why no one had bothered to adjust it.

'Ah yes, take it all in, my dear boy!' Hamilton gave Jackson a hearty slap upon his back. 'Why, this will be all yours one day!'

Hamilton drifted off to gossip with a woman standing nearby while Jackson's stomach fluttered; he handed the binoculars back to Herbert, who smirked. 'Oh yes, Cousin, I quite forgot. You've never actually *seen* a sky whale before, have you? Not in real life.'

'You've never seen your own sky whale?' Zeina exclaimed so loudly that several passengers near them turned to stare.

'No,' Jackson admitted, a heat pricking up his neck and cheeks.

'But it's your whale!'

A small girl next to them put her hand over her mouth in an attempt to hide a giggle. Jackson wanted a large hole to open up in the deck and swallow Zeina whole.

He wasn't sure what to say. "I don't really know my parents" was bound to sound ridiculous to someone like Zeina; even from the brief occasion he had seen them together, it was obvious how much she and her father loved each other.

'I prefer spending my time in Ravenport, that's all,' he said eventually. The fact that this was true did nothing to comfort Jackson from the real reason he'd never visited the whale before: after his first disastrous trip aboard an airship, his parents had never bothered to take him again. In fact, they rarely bothered to come and see him at all. When they did visit Ravenport, he'd be dressed and polished by Mrs Hogwood, just like the rest of the apartment, and then presented to them at an evening party or grand dinner. Usually by the time pudding was served he had already been ushered up to bed and then, in the morning, they'd be gone again, off on another holiday for months. He gulped, eyes prickling as a knot formed in his throat.

Zeina let out a long, exasperated sigh. 'If I had my own sky whale I wouldn't be wasting any time down in Ravenport, that's for sure. I'd be up here all the time.'

'Well, you two can explore together, can't you? Don't worry, we have maps and signposts everywhere and plenty of stewards around to help first-time passengers, so you shouldn't get lost.' There was a smug look on Herbert's face, which made Jackson want to push him overboard.

CHAPTER 9

I t was all Zeina could do not to squeal with excitement, her heart dancing as she watched the whale grow closer. Finally, after so many hours of dreaming, she was seeing one up-close in real life! Shielding her eyes from the rising sun, she leaned over the railings in order to get the best possible view.

The hotel glistened, gold and glass gleaming in the morning light. The buildings were all different shapes and styles yet seemed to work together somehow. A magnificent dome shone like a jewel at one end, while elegant steeples cut dagger shapes into the sky at the other. There were balconies and turrets and archways all built upon a metal shell around the whale's middle. Across sweeping terraces were gardens complete with statues and trees, lush and green in comparison to the withered little things left in Ravenport. Tiny insect-like airships buzzed to and from the many platforms, clouds of steam spiralled from the funnels near the tail and it was all larger and more impressive than Zeina could have ever imagined.

Seeing a real sky whale in the flesh filled Zeina's head with questions she had never before considered. How did they actually go about catching one of these giant beasts? How do they even begin to build the hotels? What does the STAN system do, exactly, in order to keep them so calm? The whale in front of her seemed so far from the images of vicious wild whales in her scavenged books that it seemed to be a different creature altogether; rubbery lips drawn closed over deadly teeth, a huge black eye staring blankly at nothing, all traces of rage faded into serenity.

She would have pumped Jackson for information were it not that he was in such a foul mood. He frowned, face hot, nostrils flared, and refused to look at her or anybody else.

It was about an hour before stewards appeared on deck with ropes and anchors, ready to dock. The whale was now so close that Zeina could see deep scars on the whale's flippers – battle wounds from its wild days, Hamilton told them. Men appeared at the whale's docking station with hooks and chains that hauled the *Sparrowhawk* in, anchoring it to the platform, and a team of stewards pushed a walkway up to the railings to unload luggage and passengers.

'Coming through! Out of the way!' Hamilton yelled, shepherding the children right to the front of the queue of people waiting to disembark. 'Really, we *must* be first off! You there,' he pointed to a quivering steward, 'go and find our luggage immediately and do be careful. I have suits in there worth more than your year's earnings and if there's any damage I'll be sure to have you thrown overboard. Ha-ha tee-hee!'

The little steward went pale and rather sweaty and then scurried away towards the cargo hold.

'My stewards do love my little jokes, you know!' Hamilton turned to Zeina. 'Come now! This way!'

A crowd had formed on the platform to watch the *Sparrowhawk* arrive. The flashes of press photographers' cameras blinded Zeina as they descended the walkway and were followed by a barrage of questions.

'Jackson, how does it feel to be here at last?'

'Hamilton, when will Jackson be moving here permanently?'

'Are you worried about the recent reports of Smog Rat attacks?'

Through the bustling crowd, Zeina saw a curious figure looming above the heads of the others. It was tall – much taller even than her dad, who was one of the tallest people in Willoughby Towers – and although it was shrouded in a dark cloak, she was certain she spotted the outline of two furry ears pointing out of a gloomy hood. A camera near the front made her see stars for a second and, with the swish of a cape and a flash of whiskers, the mysterious figure had gone. She vowed to investigate when she could; the non-humans that they shared the continents with were just another thing Zeina was desperate to find out about.

Hamilton paused only briefly to smile for photos before marching the children from the busy platform. Within seconds, a lift transported them into the gleaming grandness of the hotel lobby, where light poured into an opulent atrium through an enormous domed skylight. The walls were at least six storeys tall and were panelled floor-to-ceiling in rich mahogany. Stewards wheeled luggage trolleys across the marble floor towards the reception desk, where rows of keys rested on golden hooks. Beaming receptionists greeted the guests and called instructions to porters. In the centre was an enormous statue of Jackson's grandfather holding a marble sky whale above his head. Water spilled from the whale's mouth in a waterfall, and surrounding the fountain's base was an array of vibrant plants, the likes of which Zeina had never seen before.

'The plants were collected by a dear friend of mine, Miss Aurelia Addle, the famous botanist,' said Hamilton. 'Transported by her personally from the different continents, a demonstration of each new land claimed in the Willoughby name. Excellent to see them growing so well up here, away from all that nasty smog!'

Although the display of succulent leaves and radiant flowers was striking, it seemed unfair to Zeina that the

Willoughbys could simply claim whatever land they wanted, especially when she thought of the Belows all living stacked on top of one another in the grey towers of Ravenport. Many of them would only ever get to see flowers like this if they were arranging them in a vase for an Above's sitting room.

Before she could think of anything to say, Hamilton sped them towards a huge double staircase complete with a pair of roaring lion sculptures. Marble steps with curved rosewood banisters led passengers up, left or right, to the first row of terraces.

'We have more facilities than any other sky whale hotel, my dears. To the left you can reach the promenade deck and from there the gymnasium, the steam room, the spa, the swimming pool, the beauty parlour, the barber shop! Oh, and the tennis courts. To the right is the lounge, the dining saloon and the library. We have two tea rooms, three restaurants and the Grand Ballroom, of course, for any special little parties of mine. Jackson, you must take Miss Starborn to our zoological gardens.' His hand rested upon the head of one of the stone lions. 'These are from the Ravenport Zoo, you know. The director sold them to me when it was shut down due to the smog. Tragic, really!' He beamed, stroking the lion's head affectionately. 'However, they do look right at home here on our grand staircase!'

Hamilton steered them towards a lift with an attendant inside.

'Good afternoon, sir.'

'Up to my suite, Barnaby, and quickly, please!'

Barnaby bowed and the lift set off. It was glass-fronted so they got a view of the lobby and of the grand staircase as it weaved up from floor to floor.

'Now, my dears, up that staircase you will find the guest rooms. They are all first class, of course, but then we also have our first-class suites and the VIP parlour rooms for our most exclusive guests.'

Zeina's eyes scanned hungrily where Hamilton was pointing. She was sure that if Miss Steele were still aboard she was bound to have a VIP cabin.

'My rooms are in the penthouse, of course,' Hamilton boasted.

'What's down there?' Zeina asked, pointing to another staircase, leading below the lobby floor.

'Oh, you should have no reason to venture down there!' he said with disdain. 'It simply leads down to the engines, luggage hold, kitchens, STANS room and the staff cabins – nothing of any interest.'

Zeina made a vow to go and check out the STANS room before she left.

'Ah, here we are. Home sweet home!' Hamilton flung his arms open wide as they entered his penthouse.

Zeina got the distinct feeling that Hamilton had designed

much of his sitting room himself. Beside a majestic fireplace were a number of sumptuous settees and an array of high-backed armchairs, each covered in a different shade of bright velvet. There were at least five statues, two fountains and an assortment of stuffed dead animals in glass cases. Above the mantle hung a giant portrait of Hamilton and Herbert in a gold frame, and any spare bit of floor space was covered in animal-skin rugs – golden-spotted ones, hairy brown ones and what Zeina thought looked like the skin of an extinct striped cat.

'Your cabins are in the East Wing, my dears. The maids will assist you with anything you need. I'm out for dinner tonight but Chef will prepare whatever takes your fancy. Herbert will dine with you, won't you, dear?'

'Oh, Father, you forget that my chest,' he forced out another pitiful cough, 'can sometimes take a day or two.'

'Oh, of course, my dearest! Martha? Martha!'

A sullen-looking maid arrived.

'Martha, fetch Herbert some hot chocolate, will you?' He tickled Herbert under the chin as you would a cat. 'Go and rest, my dear. Martha won't be long with your drink.'

Zeina thought she noticed a distinct eye-roll from the maid before she disappeared.

'Goodness me, look at the time!' Hamilton said, squinting through his monocle at his pocket watch. 'Goodbye, my dears! Have fun exploring and do take care of Miss Starborn, Jackson.'

With that he left, and Zeina and Jackson collapsed, bewildered, on to one of the luminous settees.

Zeina attempted to break the silence. 'Your uncle and cousin are . . .'

'Awful,' Jackson said miserably.

'No, no, they're friendly and . . .' she looked around her for inspiration, 'stylish?'

Jackson snorted with laughter, throwing one of the dreadful velvet cushions at her head.

'Hey!' Zeina dodged, brows furrowed. 'I was trying to be polite!'

'Well, you're terrible at it,' Jackson replied, but at least he was smiling now. If she was going to be stuck with him for the next few days, she couldn't stand the thought of dragging him round with a face like thunder.

'Come on then, rich boy,' she teased. 'Some of us haven't got a whole lifetime to spend exploring sky whales – a few days are all I've got!' With a groan, he allowed her to pull him up, push him out of the door and back to the lift. Despite being stuck with Jackson Willoughby, Zeina's whole body hummed with excitement. This was what she had been waiting for her entire life.

CHAPTER 10

Jackson was largely left to entertain Zeina himself during the first days of their trip. They barely saw Hamilton, who spent much of his time attending brunches, luncheons and afternoon tea parties, only stopping by his penthouse to change into a new outfit. Often he'd be out until the early hours of the morning and not appear from his quarters until at least midday.

Neither did they see much of Herbert, for it seemed that whenever Jackson or Zeina were around the sitting room, Herbert's chest would suddenly get worse and he'd have to retire to his room.

Jackson certainly didn't miss their company, but it also meant that he was left solely in charge of Zeina, which could sometimes be like trying to manage an enthusiastically rowdy puppy.

Zeina either was unaware that she made Jackson feel uncomfortable much of the time or didn't care that she did.

Despite the open-air decks making him woozy, she dragged him up and down every one so that she could examine the magnificent views. She demanded that they stuff their faces at every restaurant the Whale had to offer and insisted that they visit every single one of the attractions. Reluctantly he spent a whole morning trying (and failing) to teach Zeina how to play tennis and an afternoon showing her how to play bowls on the deck. Although Zeina did not know how to swim, she dived into the deep end of the impressive open-air swimming pool, forcing Jackson to plunge in after her and sweep her off the bottom. Unperturbed, she raced and splashed about in the shallows, diving underneath each of the marble whale-shaped fountains, until a steward suggested that perhaps they should go somewhere else.

In the reading room, Zeina was enthralled by the towering shelves of books, borrowing so many that Jackson had to ask a steward for a luggage trolley to take them back to her room. So fascinated was she by the ceiling of the Grand Lounge, where there was a giant map illustrated with all the animals and plants of the four kingdoms, that she insisted they both lay face up in the very middle of the mosaic floor, forcing a number of tutting and huffing guests to step over them. Although Jackson missed his velocycle, keeping up with Zeina kept him so busy that he had little time to think about the time trials.

Despite not actually seeing Hamilton, Jackson had the

distinct feeling that he was everywhere. Whenever Zeina or he would try to escape from the other, a "helpful" steward would always seem to guide them back together. In the end, they came to realise they were quite stuck with one another and simply gave up trying. They were also dressed for each day, Hamilton providing each of them with matching outfits, and often the press would turn up, taking sneaky pictures of them together. There were places they were encouraged to go, and places they could not. The casino, obviously, was out of bounds and so was anywhere below deck. Zeina came up with numerous ploys to get past the lobby and down to the engine room and the STANS room, yet whenever they got close, there again was a steward "helpfully" suggesting that they explore the steam room or the promenade deck instead.

On the afternoon of their third day, they went to explore the whale hotel's zoological gardens, which were full of strange plants and unusual insects that Jackson had never seen before. There were no animals left at the old Ravenport Zoo any more, apart from the odd pigeon or maybe a rat or two, and even the Above roof-top parks didn't have wild animals in them. For some reason unknown to Jackson, Zeina seemed completely enchanted by a particularly bad-tempered dragon lizard with enormous claws. Alarmingly, "Jeffrey" was allowed to roam freely, and when Zeina decided to follow him into a large tropical bush to watch him dismantle a beetle with his sharp jaws, Jackson opted to stay behind on one of the benches.

It was then that he heard a familiar voice; Herbert's unmistakeable snarky tone drifted up from the terrace below and Jackson leaned over to see who he was talking to. Herbert and a collection of friends, all wearing garish suits, were gathered around a newspaper, on the front page of which was a picture of Jackson and Zeina in matching purple outfits. He could remember the photo being snapped yesterday on the promenade deck. The headline read: **"COULD THIS BE THE FUTURE LADY WILLOUGHBY?"** and underneath in slightly smaller text, 'Heir to the Willoughby fortune, Jackson Willoughby, enjoys the company of unknown Below on his first visit to the Willoughby Whale.'

Herbert's raucous laughter rang in Jackson's ears.

'Can you imagine?' Herbert laughed. 'That girl is more feral cat than Lady!'

His friends joined in, chuckling heartily as they passed the article around.

'Oh, Herby! Really, I don't know how you bear it?' cried one of them, dabbing his eyes with a handkerchief.

'*He's* not much better,' Herbert snapped, pointing to Jackson in the picture. 'Look at him, it's obvious he's terrified. Can you imagine *him* taking over and running this place one day? *Him* instead of *me*? It's not fair!'

There was an enthusiastic murmur of agreement from his friends.

'Eurgh, I can't wait for them to go home! Land-dwellers! Honestly, the whole apartment reeks!'

'Why can't your dad send them back down where they belong? The Below, at least!' one asked.

'Don't you think I've asked? He won't! Says they've got to stay until the week is out and that's that. Doesn't matter how much I beg or cough,' Herbert sulked. 'It's the grease and the smell – she stinks! Seriously, you've got to come round and have a sniff for yourself!'

They erupted into another round of cruel laughter and Jackson turned away angrily, not wanting to hear any more.

'What are you doing?' Zeina appeared suddenly next to him. 'You look awful again – all pale and sick.'

'Oh, it's nothing. I'm just hungry, that's all. Come on, let's go back to the rooms. I'm sure Chef will cook us up some more of that treacle tart if we ask.'

This had the desired effect. Zeina nodded enthusiastically and he guided her away from the terrace as quickly as he could. Even though Zeina got on his nerves, it had nothing to do with the fact she was a Below and he an Above. Jackson felt disgusted that a member of his own family felt that way; he couldn't stand the thought of Zeina hearing Herbert and his friends and assuming he thought like them too.

CHAPTER 11

After a mountain of treacle tart, Zeina returned to her room to find two notes waiting for her. The one dotted with smudged black fingerprints she tore open first and was greeted by Shrapnel's lumpy handwriting.

> ZEE,
> STAYIN ABOARD THIS EVE.
> SNEAK BELOW DECK AFTER MIDNIGHT.
> COME IN OVERALLS. ASK FOR ME.
> SHRAP X

She was relieved. Not only was she desperate to tell him all about her trip, but he would also be able to tell her exactly how much trouble she was in back at home. So far she had successfully managed to block out the thought of facing her dad when she returned to Ravenport, but now, with only one day left, the fear was beginning to keep her up at night.

The other note was in a baby-blue envelope that smelled curiously of flowers and sugar.

Miss Zeina Starborn

YOU ARE CORDIALLY INVITED TO

The Willoughby Whale's

15TH ANNUAL SUMMER BALL

GRAND BALLROOM
AT 2 P.M.

❦ DRESS CODE: FORMAL EVENING WEAR ❦

She had been beginning to wonder if Hamilton had forgotten that part of her prize was to meet Vivianne Steele, but this must be it! Despite dragging Jackson all over the Whale, she had caught no glimpse of the famous explorer since they arrived. Hamilton had promised they would meet Miss Steele at the Summer Ball — and it was tonight! She squealed, jumping out of her seat and clapping her hands together.

She would wait until after the ball finished and then sneak down the lobby stairs to find Shrapnel. The thought of keeping it a secret from Jackson made her stomach twist uncomfortably. Although being stuck with him all week

82

hadn't been quite as bad as she had expected, she could only imagine the look on Shrapnel's face if she turned up tonight with Jackson Willoughby in tow!

Martha entered with a cornflower-blue evening dress. Made of silk, its puffed sleeves were trimmed with ribbons, and a lavender sash separated the bodice from the skirt. Zeina sighed, counting at least four layers of underskirts and petticoats but with Martha's help it didn't take as long to get into as she had feared. There were matching silk gloves, a sapphire brooch and a feather fan. By some miracle, Martha managed to smooth Zeina's hair into a bun, securing it with little jewelled pins.

'There you are! Told you it wouldn't take long if you held still. Don't look half bad, if I do say so myself!'

Zeina, who had been frowning while Martha struggled with her hair, now turned to face the mirror and was pleasantly surprised with what she saw. She, personally, would not have chosen the frilly neck or puffy sleeves, but she actually quite liked the colour. Vivianne Steele was always dressed in the latest fashions and Zeina wanted to look her best when she met her hero.

It was close to eight p.m. by the time Hamilton emerged from his rooms. His evening suit was a particularly ghastly shade of orange and embellished with arrangements of large tropical flowers.

'Now, don't you two look splendid! The dress fits perfectly, I see, Miss Starborn. And look, I have styled you two to match!' Jackson's pink cheeks clashed horribly with his turquoise hat. 'My dear friend, Miss Addle, flew in from the Southern Continent this morning with the flowers – freshly cut. Do you think they are too much?' Hamilton asked as he regarded himself in an ornately decorated hand mirror.

'No, Uncle. They are lovely, really. Very bright and, um . . . tasteful.'

Catching Jackson's smirk, Zeina had to press her lips together to stop herself from giggling.

'Fantastic! I have an arrangement each for the both of you too!'

Jackson's face fell as Hamilton magicked a rainbow of blue and purple blooms for the brim of Jackson's hat and another for Zeina to wear around her wrist.

Zeina noticed a twitch of anger in Jackson's eyes as Herbert entered wearing a tangerine ensemble with the same enormous tropical embellishments as his father. Behind him was Martha, carrying an elaborate gold cage.

'Where would you like this, Mr Hamilton?'

'Oh, Jackson will carry it, won't you, dear? Can't ask Herbert; the feathers aren't good for his allergies.'

Perched inside the cage was the most extraordinary bird

Zeina had ever seen. White-beaked and dark-eyed, its iridescent silvery feathers looked as if they were made of glass. It hopped angrily from one white-clawed foot to the other, letting out low, ugly croaks.

'Ah, Miss Starborn, I see you are quite taken with little Albi. Delivered this afternoon by Sir Claringbold, a most prestigious zoologist who specialises in rare birds from the Northern Continent.'

Hamilton opened a spotted handkerchief and pushed what looked like leftover cake from that afternoon's tea through the bars of Albi's gilded cage. Although the bird gobbled down the crumbs greedily, something about his beady black eyes made Zeina think that he would probably have quite enjoyed snapping off one of Hamilton's fingers instead.

'What is it?' asked Jackson, holding the cage as far from his face as his arm would stretch.

'Ah, Jackson, *Corvus albineus* – or the Ice Raven – is really the most extraordinary and *expensive* of specimens. Those feathers reflect light in such a way that they are completely invisible in flight. Excellent messenger birds – they can fly from the darkest corners of the Northern Continent to the Southern Border in a matter of hours! No more than a handful of people on this continent will have ever seen one in real life. He's going to help us make our grand entrance, aren't you, little Albi.' He put on the same baby voice he did sometimes when he was talking to Herbert, making Albi snap and croak loudly in Hamilton's face. He sighed. 'Oh, Albi, how I would love to keep you for our zoological gardens, but alas, you are a gift for our guest of honour this evening. Miss Starborn, you must be quite excited about finally meeting the famous Vivianne Steele?'

'I can't wait, Mr Willoughby. Thank you so much for allowing me to come.' Her heart raced with anticipation and she was pleased with herself for remembering her manners. Jackson raised an eyebrow.

✷

Zeina had been impressed with the decorations at Jackson's party, but nothing could have prepared her for the Grand Ballroom that evening; every inch was covered in tropical flowers. Bright garlands were weaved around every pillar, swathed around every banister and suspended from every one of the dazzling electric chandeliers. They formed enormous centrepieces around golden candelabras on every table and were tied around every golden chair. In the centre of a buffet table, surrounded by platters of meats and cheeses, towers of pies and tarts, an arrangement of lobster tails and crab claws, and mountains of fruits and cakes, was an enormous ice sculpture of Hamilton himself, complete with a giant icy top hat adorned with exotic plants. Behind the stage, where a string quartet played gentle music, flowers hung in a curtain from ceiling to floor. From the balcony, Zeina thought the crowd of guests looked like a sea of flowers, all wearing bright suits or huge dresses with frills that stuck out like petals.

Hamilton opened the lock of Albi's cage and coaxed out the bird, using more leftover cake.

'Take the cage down to the display stand,' Hamilton hissed to a steward, looking rather nervously at the sleeve of his suit, where Albi stood.

The herald's booming voice stopped the band, cutting through the chatter to announce their entrance.

'LADIES AND GENTLEMEN! May I present your most gracious host for this evening, Mr Hamilton Willoughby!'

There was a round of applause and cheering as Hamilton bowed.

'His most honoured nephew and heir to the Willoughby fortune, Master Jackson Willoughby,' more clapping followed, 'and his son, Master Herbert Willoughby.'

Another round of applause echoed around the ballroom.

'And Miss Zeina Starborn of Ravenport.'

The clapping was noticeably quieter, as some guests whispered to each other.

'As a special treat this evening, most honoured guests, may I also introduce to you a spectacle never before seen on this continent, The Ice Raven!'

Hamilton lifted the arm holding Albi up over the balcony railing and, although he squawked and snapped a little at first, the bird soon took off, flying elegantly over the heads of the silent crowd. In flight he was transformed – a flash, a gleam, a graceful soaring light – re-emerging into the silvery bird only when he landed back on the perch of his cage, to enraptured applause.

'Ah ha! Quite the crowd-pleaser!' Hamilton beamed. 'Now, my dears, Herbert and I have a few people we must catch up with. You don't mind entertaining yourselves, do you? We'll get all the boring mingling out of the way and you can join us later.'

'Jackson could take Miss Starborn to the buffet table, Father. Chef tells me how much she loves our food. She should enjoy it while she can, don't you think?'

Despite Herbert's warm, bright voice, Zeina felt as if her face had been slapped by an icy palm.

'Capital idea! My Herbert is always so thoughtful! Enjoy yourselves, my dears!'

Hamilton whisked himself and Herbert away before they could answer. Jackson stared moodily after them.

'I'm . . . I'm not like them. You do know that, don't you?' he asked, turning to face Zeina, his eyes wide and his face flushed.

'I know,' Zeina was about to answer, when she saw something that made her stop dead. 'Jackson,' she whispered. '*Look!*'

He followed her gaze, eyes locking immediately on a tall man surrounded by a throng of adoring fans.

'It's Franklyn Beaumont! The *real* Franklyn Beaumont! Come on – he's your hero! You should introduce yourself.' She grabbed Jackson's hand and pulled.

'I . . . I can't . . . I . .' he stammered, frozen to the spot.

'Oh, c'mon! Why are you always so afraid of everything?' She shoved him to the front, waving her hand in the air and shouting, 'Franklyn, Franklyn! This is Jackson! He's your biggest fan!'

Franklyn turned towards them, for it was hard to ignore Zeina once she had decided she wanted your attention.

'Hey there!' He smiled handsomely, holding out his hand. 'Always great to meet a fan. Tell me, do you ride?'

'Um.' Jackson held his hero's hand and gazed up, captivated and speechless.

Zeina sighed. 'Yes, he *does*. He never shuts up about velocycles usually! He's going to your time trials next week.'

'Oh, great! I'll see you there! It's Jackson, isn't it?'

Franklyn got a pen and a piece of card out of his pocket and began writing.

'There you go, Jackson! You can keep this in your pocket for luck.'

Franklyn and his mob drifted away, and Jackson was left clutching the little card. He and Zeina stared at it, Franklyn Beaumont's handsome face smiling back.

Jackson
See you at the time trials - good luck!
Franklyn X

'This is the best thing I've ever been given,' he breathed.

'What? That little photograph is better than all those enormous expensive presents you get every year?' She laughed. 'It means you definitely have to go now. No chickening out!'

'I will,' murmured Jackson in reply, a grin spreading over his face. And just for a moment he looked so ridiculously happy, so un-Jackson-like, that Zeina could have hugged him.

'Now, here are some people I have been most anxious to meet, Katu.'

A charming voice made them whirl round. The person who greeted them was one of the most beautiful women Zeina had ever seen. Dressed head to toe in fitted velvet the colour of midnight, her auburn curls cascaded from under a silk high-crowned hat. Around her throat a choker glittered with diamonds and her emerald eyes sparkled.

'I am honoured to meet you, my dears. Miss Vivianne Steele at your service.'

She offered her hand to Zeina and Jackson in turn. It was Zeina's turn to freeze now, staring up at her hero. Butterflies danced in her stomach and she was very glad for her gloves, as her palms began to sweat.

'I . . . I . . . I've wanted to meet you for . . . for ever,' she stuttered.

Vivianne laughed softly. 'Well, I too have wanted to meet *you* for some time. Hamilton wrote to ask me to come to the ball to meet you both. I've been on an expedition these last few days, but Katu here, my Chief Navigator, has told me you have made quite the impression!'

It was only now that Zeina really looked at the figure standing next to Vivianne. So fascinated was she by her hero that she hadn't noticed that her companion wasn't human at all. Although he stood taller than a man and was wearing a fine suit like all the other gentlemen at the party, under his top hat, his face was a mixture of cat and bear. He bowed low now, removing his hat to reveal two brown pointed ears that Zeina was certain she had glimpsed before.

'Lovely to meet you, Master Willoughby, and you too . . . Miss Zeina.'

When he spoke, Zeina noticed the rows of sharp white teeth below his whiskers – and was it her imagination or had there been a distinct coolness to his tone when he said her name?

'Now, Katu,' Vivianne said rather deliberately, 'go back and check on the crew for me, please. They'll have finished unloading by now and will be up to all kinds of mischief, I'm sure.' She turned her dazzling smile on Jackson. 'Master Willoughby, you wouldn't mind going to locate your lovely uncle for me, would you? There are some matters I need to discuss with him, and it will give me a chance to chat to Zeina here.'

Jackson didn't seem to want to leave Miss Steele, but nevertheless he did as he was told, and Zeina was left alone with the legendary explorer.

'Now, my dear Zeina. May I call you Zeina? You may call me Vivianne, of course. All my friends call me Vivianne or Viv and I just get the feeling that we will be great friends!' Zeina felt rather woozy as her heart swelled in her chest. She was glad when Vivianne linked arms with her to lead her gently to a pair of chairs.

'Well, Zeina, firstly please don't mind Katu. He is an excellent navigator but such a horrible snob. He can't help it, really! The eldest of the Kotarth princes – and they have fallen on hard times, poor things! Despite his bad manners, we are most lucky. I don't know any other airship with a Kotarth navigator. Have you ever seen a Kotarth before?'

Zeina could do nothing but shake her head as Vivianne waved over a waitress carrying a tray of drinks. 'A wonderful species, the Kotarth. They have senses we don't and can communicate with most animals across great distances. He's fantastic at tracking sky whales for me, although his communication skills with humans sometimes leave a little to be desired! Oh, are you all right, dear?'

Zeina hadn't tried sitting down in her dress yet and it was causing her some difficulty. Holding a drink in one hand and being unaccustomed to the layers of underskirt, the fabric kept getting bunched up behind her, causing her to slide off her chair.

'Here you go, dear,' smiled Vivianne kindly, taking hold of Zeina's drink so she could hop up. 'Not used to wearing evening dresses, I suppose?'

'No, Miss St—I mean Vivianne. I'm a Below. My dad is the Willoughbys' engineer.' Zeina flushed.

'Oh, no need to be embarrassed about that! Why, it's something to be proud of. You've got the whole of the Willoughby Whale talking about you!'

'I have?' Zeina frowned.

'Of course! Do you know that I too was once a Below? Still am, I suppose! Just a Below who now gets invited to all the Above parties. These lot,' she waved at the guests, many of whom were doing little to hide the fact that they were all watching Zeina and Miss Steele, 'they seem to forget all about who your father or mother were just as soon as you start making them money!'

Zeina was astonished. In all the stories she had read about the famous Miss Steele, in all the newspaper articles that were pinned to her bedroom wall, not a single one had mentioned this fact. It was unheard of for a Below to even own an airship, yet somehow Vivianne had bought the *Raven*, built up her crew and become the most famous explorer in the history of the four continents.

'But . . . how?' Zeina's head buzzed with a million questions.

'Why, you just have to know what you want and work hard. Grab opportunities and make the most of them! Does that sound like something you would like to do, my dear?'

Zeina thought about her dad, who worked hard every day of his life, fixing the airships of a family who didn't even know his name. She thought about smog and respirators and service lifts and school lessons on following instructions. Vivianne made it sound easy, but the fact was that a day from now she would be returning to Ravenport and she would most likely never see the Upper Atmosphere again.

'I go back home to Ravenport tomorrow. I'm to start my apprenticeship with my dad in a few months – he needs help with the airships.'

'Ah well, I'm sure you will be a really excellent engineer one day! And how lovely to work side by side with your father,' she smiled, her eyes sparkling with mischief. 'It's a shame you can't enjoy a little adventure first though. See what opportunities arise?'

Zeina's head felt foggy. What did she mean?

'Now, do you think your father would be able to manage another week or so without you?'

Zeina nodded, unsure but unable to do or say anything else.

'Leave it to me, dear,' she whispered with a grin, patting Zeina's arm. 'Hamilton!' She stood up and put out her hand to Hamilton, who was hurrying over to them, Jackson and Herbert in tow. He grabbed her hand, bending low to kiss it, which made Zeina feel a little queasy.

'Vivianne! You look wonderful! No – fabulous! No – breathtaking! As always!'

'You are too kind, Hamilton. Zeina and I have just been talking about you. How kind you are to have given her this opportunity. A trip of a lifetime! And you are such a fabulous host.' She gestured at the decorations. 'I have just been telling her that no one throws a party like Hamilton!'

Zeina was impressed at how easily Vivianne could lie. Jackson's eyebrows raised sceptically but Hamilton was eating up the praise, beaming and blushing under his enormous hat.

'Now, I have just had the most fabulous idea!' She stroked his arm, making him turn an even deeper shade of red. 'I have been thinking that your lovely Jackson here should come along with me and my crew for the trip. What an amazing experience for the boy whose grandfather captured the first sky whale! He can be your ambassador of sorts; check that I am completing the job to the full satisfaction of the Willoughby family.'

The colour drained rapidly from Jackson's face as Hamilton twirled his moustache in consideration. 'Oh, and Miss Starborn could come along, of course,' she continued casually, making it sound like an afterthought. 'An extra little treat. Away from all that smog for a bit longer before returning to Ravenport. Good for her lungs.'

'Uncle?' Jackson questioned, but Hamilton ignored him, tapping one finger on pursed lips.

'Hmm . . . Why, Miss Steele, I do believe that is an excellent idea! Jackson is to inherit all of this one day after all – and really, these sorts of trips are so much safer than they used to be.'

'Uncle Hamilton, I—' Jackson attempted but was waved away.

'Every precaution will be taken and my crew are very experienced. He will be quite safe. And Miss Starborn can come too?'

'*Uncle?*' Despite the desperation now in Jackson's voice, he was again ignored by both the adults.

'Why, yes, of course! Would you like that, my dear? Would you enjoy accompanying Jackson and Miss Steele to the Western Continent in order to capture a new sky whale for the Willoughbys?'

CHAPTER 12

Jackson drifted through the rest of the party as if he were stuck in a horrible dream.

From across the room he saw Zeina talk animatedly to Vivianne for most of the evening, but caught only snippets of Steele's replies.

'. . . First thing tomorrow morning . . .'

'. . . Northern Outpost of Wren . . . Ragrock Falls . . . over the Western Mountains . . .'

'. . . Yes, my dear, quite the adventure . . .'

An anger was bubbling up inside him like lava, and soon he would have no control over it.

Zeina's high spirits persisted when they left the ball and made their way back to the penthouse, asking Hamilton question after question about their trip.

Hamilton answered them as best and as quickly as he could. 'Yes, of course we shall let your father know, my dear. I will arrange a telegram so no need to worry about that now.

I'm sure he won't mind, and you are unlikely to be away longer than a week, I would judge. Back before he knows it! That's so long as there aren't any thunder-fog storms or Smog Rat sightings but I'm sure all will be fine. Miss Steele is very experienced.'

Any amount of time travelling on an airship was too much for Jackson, but a week would be devastating; he would miss the time trials – the last chance he had to change his future. Zeina was the only person in the world who knew this. They had a deal and she had broken it.

'Another whale hotel will be quite the investment for the family!' Hamilton, who was almost as giddy as Zeina, added. 'Who knows – once the second Willoughby Whale is up and running, maybe Jackson and I could name a ballroom or a suite of rooms after you, Zeina? The Starborn Suite has quite a nice ring to it!'

'Shouldn't I go on the trip with Miss Steele, instead of Miss Starborn?' Herbert whined as they headed back to their rooms after the party. '*I* am a Willoughby, after all.'

'Don't be ridiculous, Herbert! A journey over the Western Mining Grounds would be quite fatal to you, I'm sure! More to the point, you are needed here. It is the last week of the summer season and I can't possibly attend all the social engagements alone. No, Miss Starborn is much better suited to the trip and she was personally invited by Miss Steele.'

Hamilton squeezed her face as you would a small child and, for once, Zeina didn't seem to mind at all.

As soon as they entered the penthouse, Herbert slunk off to his room without saying a word to anyone. Hamilton bid them goodnight and Zeina and Jackson were left alone for the first time since they had met Vivianne.

'I can't wait to see the look on old Hoggy's face when she finds out about the Starborn Suite,' Zeina said, breaking the silence. Jackson kept his eyes firmly on the striped rug.

'Jackson, whatever is the matter?' she demanded, elbowing him in the ribs. 'I know you're not the greatest fan of airships but come on! A trip to the Western Continent. A trip with Vivianne Steele in her airship! A trip to capture a sky whale. It's going to be amazing!'

Jackson stood up. For a moment he thought he might just walk away but Zeina wasn't finished.

'And to think last week neither of us had ever even left boring old Ravenport.' Her nose crinkled as she mentioned their home and, unable to contain himself any longer, Jackson turned to face her.

'But I *wanted* to go back to boring old Ravenport, *remember*? I *wanted* to go to the time trials. We had a deal and *you* broke it!' He threw the signed photo of Franklyn down on the table. Beaumont's face smiled back at them, the gold good-luck message glinting in the light of the fire.

'Oh,' Zeina gulped, face flushing.

'But you won't have even thought about that,' Jackson spat. 'The only person you ever think about is *yourself*!'

Her fiery eyes focused on his, her tone chilled by an icy anger. 'Well, maybe if I had servants and parties and presents and airships and *my own* sky whale, maybe then I wouldn't have to think about myself all the time. Ravenport might not be boring to you but if you knew you'd be stuck there your whole life, you would think differently. Some of us have nothing to look forward to – nothing but working every day alongside Dad, doing the same job, day after day, for a family who don't even know we exist. Spoilt little rich boy. You'll never know how lucky you are.'

Her words struck Jackson like missiles but he stood his ground, desperate not to let her see how much she had hurt him.

'It's you who doesn't know how lucky you are. You have a dad who loves you, who cares about what happens to you, who . . . wants to spend time with you.' Jackson choked as his voice started to wobble. 'I bet you haven't even thought about him, waiting for you in Ravenport. How is he going to feel when he gets Hamilton's telegram, finds out that you've gone off without his permission, *again*?'

Zeina crossed her arms, shifting her eyes to stare into the dying fire. 'You're not worried about me or my dad. The only person you're worried about is yourself. You're scared, just like you always are of everything. An Above who hasn't even been to the Upper Atmosphere before? Pathetic!' she spat. 'My dad won't be worried when he knows I'm with Vivianne. You heard what Hamilton said – it's quite safe.'

Jackson laughed. 'You're an idiot if you trust anything Hamilton says!' He frowned, something that had been niggling at the back of his brain coming to the forefront. 'Why would Steele want us to go along anyway? It was arranged so quickly too. There's something about it that feels weird.'

'It's *Vivianne Steele*, Jackson!' Zeina exploded. 'She's world famous – the greatest explorer of all time!' She squared up to him, scowling, fists clenching and unclenching. 'I know what this is – you're jealous! That's it! You're jealous! She's famous and important and she was interested in *me*. She wants me to go because she knows I won't get the chance again.' Jackson noticed angry tears welling up in her eyes. 'You're just a snob – like all Aboves! You think I don't know what Herbert, what all of you, really think about me? You didn't know that Vivianne was a Below until tonight and now you don't trust her because you think you're better than us!'

Molten anger raged within him. How dare she say he was like Herbert?

'I don't care about either of you being Belows! And I've

been nothing but polite to you! It was *you* who broke our deal. The only thing you care about is getting your own way.'

Zeina turned away from him, arms folded, silent for once.

'Somehow you've managed to sign us both up for your dream trip. One that's not only extremely dangerous but also means *my* dream is over. The Ravenport Racers won't have their next trials for another year and by then, my parents will have made me move up here. Next week was my last chance and you knew that!'

Zeina remained statue-still, refusing to look at him. Jackson's head throbbed – there was no point, nothing else he could do.

'You don't care about me, you don't care about keeping promises, you don't even care about your dad. You're selfish and I hate that I'm stuck with you.'

And with that he stomped off, slamming the door to his room behind him.

CHAPTER 13

As the grandfather clock in the darkened lobby struck one, Zeina emerged below deck. It had taken her much longer than she had anticipated to struggle out of her ridiculous dress, into her overalls and then out of the apartment and down to the service lift without being seen.

It was silent below deck, save for the distant hum of machinery. There were no gold fountains, exotic plants or marble floors, just metal corridors, pipes and ore fumes, and in an instant Zeina felt right at home. The pounding of her heart eased a little but the fight with Jackson still rang in her ears. How dare he say those things about her? Shrapnel would understand. *He* would be excited about the trip, even if Jackson wasn't, and he could get the letter she had written back to her dad. The guilt she felt about Jackson missing the time trials ebbed and flowed, but when she thought about her dad getting that telegram from Hamilton a horrible heaviness struck the depths of her stomach. She hated to admit it, but Jackson was right – her dad would be beside himself with worry. She bit her lip, fingering the letter, which was stuffed into the pocket of her overalls. It explained what had happened, why she had to go and told him not to worry and that she loved him.

Shrapnel's note hadn't said exactly where she should go once she got below deck; it simply said 'ASK FOR ME'. In the distance, there was a rhythmic clanking and the murmur of deep voices. They reminded her of the sound an airship made when it was getting ready to depart and she set off in that direction.

The clanking grew louder, the corridor hotter and murmurs became shouts. A faint orange glow filled the passage and Zeina had to loosen her overalls and wipe sweat from her brow. She turned a corner and saw the source of the noise. It was the engine room, just as she had suspected. The window in the steel door radiated a bright, red heat. Peeking in, she could see never-ending rows of furnaces, with engine crew working tirelessly, shovelling mountains of ore into the flames. The largest of the Willoughby airships had five furnaces, but in this engine room there were at least a hundred.

Zeina's hand was on the handle of the door when something else caught her eye. The bright glow coming off the window had illuminated another door in the gloom of the passageway. Covered top to bottom in locks and bolts, it was larger and thicker than the door of the engine room and possessed a tiny hatch at about the height of an adult's eyeline. A mysterious low buzzing drew her towards it.

Tall for her age, Zeina still had to stand on tiptoes, fingers gripping one of the bolts, and pull herself up to slide open the hatch and peer through the tiny peephole underneath. She caught a glimpse of white coats, wires, glowing buttons and the buzz of electric lights, before she was grabbed roughly from behind.

'And who might you be?'

Her blood ran cold as she recognised the unmistakeable dark-green lawkeeper uniforms. The one holding Zeina's arms behind her back was tall and lanky, while the other, shorter and broader, held a truncheon to lift up her chin and a gas lantern to illuminate her face.

'I said, WHO might you be?' he repeated, smiling cruelly at her.

'Um . . . My name is Zeina Starborn. I was looking for my friend, Shrapnel. He's engine-room crew for the Willoughby fleet.'

'Shrapnel? Never heard of him! Sounds made up, doesn't it, Lester?'

'It does, Joe. It does.'

Joe's lantern was beginning to burn an angry redness across her cheek.

'Where are your papers?'

'Papers? I don't have papers! I'm here as a guest of Jackson Willoughby.'

One look at her grease-stained overalls sent both the lawkeepers into raucous laughter.

'Oh, that's a good one! A new one for us, isn't it, Lester? I don't believe for one second that any of the Willoughbys would lower themselves to be friends with the likes of you! Come on. The truth now.' Joe's tone became sharp; he wasn't laughing any more.

'I'm telling the truth! I'm here as a guest of Jackson and Hamilton Willoughby. Guests don't need papers!'

'You're a stowaway? A runaway from the ore mines? A Smog Rat scout? Why else would you be snooping round the STANS room at night?'

'Don't matter, Joe. Anyone down here without papers gets sent to the mines anyway.'

A wave of panic swept through Zeina. Nobody even knew she was here.

'Yeah but Smog Rats I like to rough up a bit first,' he said, an evil grin spreading across his face.

'HEY!'

Zeina was relieved to hear Shrapnel's frantic voice. From the corner of her eye she saw him running down the passageway towards them. 'She's telling the truth! I'm Shrapnel – engine crew from the *Sparrowhawk*. I have my papers here.'

Joe grunted, disappointed to have to remove the truncheon from Zeina's chin and lower the gas lantern in order to examine the papers Shrapnel flapped in his face.

He shrugged. 'So you are who you say you are. Doesn't matter! This one,' he pressed the lantern maliciously into Zeina's nose, 'has no papers and our orders are very clear, aren't they, Lester?'

'They are, Joe. Very clear. She needs arresting and taking to head office where she'll be deported to the ore mines.'

'What about your orders to guard the STANS room at all times then?' Shrapnel said. 'I'm sure Mr Willoughby will want to hear that it was left unguarded, AT NIGHT, when we're all on high alert. Was that the idea of you coming down here, Miss Starborn? How many lawkeepers were here when you arrived?'

'Um . . . Oh! Not one, Mr Shrapnel. Not one!' Zeina caught on, putting on her haughtiest Mrs Hogwood voice. 'I'm sure Mr Willoughby will be very interested to hear that no one was here when I arrived to, uh . . . inspect the STANS room.'

Lester gulped, loosening his grip on Zeina's arm. He and Joe frowned at each other for a moment, silently debating what to do next, and then Joe sighed heavily.

'Say we let you go,' he began slowly. 'Say you were to tell Mr Hamilton that we arrived as soon as you approached the STANS room door? You see, just a few minutes before, Lester had heard something suspicious, hadn't you, Lester?'

'That's right, Joe.'

'Yes, Lester had heard something suspicious down the corridor and we had gone to investigate. As you say, Mr Shrapnel, we must all be on high alert, especially at night.'

'Yes, I see. I'm sure Mr Hamilton and Master Jackson would be only too pleased to hear that you take your duties so seriously, wouldn't they, Miss Starborn?'

'Yes, Mr Shrapnel, indeed.'

Lester let go of Zeina completely as Joe reluctantly replaced his truncheon on his belt. Scowling, Zeina straightened her overalls and rubbed her sore chin.

'No hard feelings, I hope, Miss Starborn. In these times I'm sure any *personal friend* of the Willoughbys understands that we must be vigilant.'

Lester's lip curled into a sneer.

'Come on now, Miss Starborn,' said Shrapnel, grabbing Zeina by the elbow. 'I shall escort you back to the lobby.'

Shrapnel marched Zeina away from the STANS room, remaining silent and keeping hold of her until they had got right past the service lift and down the corridor leading in the opposite direction. This corridor had cabins all along it. Some were dark and quiet, save for the occasional snore, while others were lit by flickering gaslights and crammed full of chattering people eating all manner of things, drinking out of little tin mugs and playing cards. In one room someone was even playing a trumpet. The music drifted out into the corridor, as did the throng of people dancing, clapping and tunelessly singing along.

Only when they reached the canteen at the end of the corridor did Shrapnel release Zeina and usher her to a table in a deserted corner. He poured them some tea from the hatch and handed Zeina a steaming mug.

'What in the world were you doing hanging around the STANS room?' Shrapnel spoke through clenched teeth.

'I didn't know that *was* the STANS room! I was looking for *you*!'

She considered the white coats, the tiny peephole and all those rows of electric buttons, wishing she'd had a chance to get a better look at the machinery that tamed and controlled the sky whales.

'Looking for me behind a large, suspicious-looking, bolted door? It's not safe wandering around there by yourself, especially with no papers.'

'Well, you told me to ask for you but there was no one to ask.'

'You had just passed the engine room!'

Zeina did not have an answer for this.

'Why do they need all those furnaces anyway?' she asked, eager to change topic. 'I thought the Whale flew itself?'

'It does, but those furnaces power the electrical system for the Whale and the STANS room. The STANS room requires a *lot* of power.'

'Why? What's in there? How does it control the—'

'Sshh!' he interrupted sharply, voice lowered. 'It's best not to ask too many questions, Zeina. In case you couldn't tell from all the locks on the door, it's all top secret.'

Zeina blushed but then gathered herself. 'Oh, Shrap, I've got such exciting news.'

She was pleased to see Shrapnel's mouth fall open as she told him about Vivianne's offer.

'Isn't it amazing? I never thought I'd get to go on a trip like this. I just need you to get this letter to my dad.' She presented him with the letter from her pocket. 'Hamilton is sending a telegram but this will explain better. I don't want him to worry or be angry or anything like that. You can get it to him, can't you?'

Shrapnel didn't take the letter. Instead, he put his head in his hands. 'Oh, Zee.'

'What?'

Shrapnel's face had paled and his brow furrowed. She had never seen him look so serious.

'Did no part of you think that perhaps you should just go home and say sorry to your dad? That maybe, especially after how you boarded the *Sparrowhawk* in the first place, it would be best if you *didn't* draw any more attention to yourself?'

'What? Do you mean . . . my aerocycle? How do *you* know about that?' Zeina hadn't thought much more about her new invention; it was back in her cabin, hidden in her pack. She had been too busy having fun on the Whale to even consider it since arriving.

'*Everyone* knows about that, Zee! Down here it's been the talk of the Whale! You can't just fly a mysterious new contraption up to the deck of an airship without people noticing. It's dangerous!'

'It's not! It worked perfectly!'

'I don't mean that.' Shrapnel sighed, looking around them to check they were still alone. 'There are things you don't understand yet, Zee. And I can't go into all of it now. But new technology like that – it's suspicious, OK? Questions will be asked if you're caught with it. The whole of the Eastern Continent is on the lookout for the Smog Rats's Innovator. You heard the lawkeepers – everyone is on edge; we're being searched all the time.'

'What are they looking for?'

'*Anything.* Anything strange that might suggest you are working for the Smog Rats as a scout or a go-between for the Innovator. Technology like that – it puts you in danger. How did you even get it?'

'I invented it!'

Shrapnel's eyebrows raised. He shook his head.

'You have to back out of this trip.'

'Back out? Why on earth would I back out?' An angry heat crept up her neck and into her cheeks. First Jackson and now Shrapnel. Why wasn't he happy for her?

'Zee, there are other things going on. I wish I could tell you more but it's not safe – not here.' He looked around again, lowering his voice to a whisper. 'Your dad is *frantic* already and I know he would *not* want you to go on this trip.'

'Well, it's too late. I'm going!' she retorted angrily. The thought of her dad being frantic steeped her in guilt – but she would not give up her dream for anything. Shrapnel rubbed at his eyes and for the first time she noticed how tired he looked.

'Listen, Zee. Listen very carefully to what I am about to say. Don't trust *anyone* – not Hamilton, not Herbert, not any of Vivianne's crew, *no one*. NOT Jackson Willoughby. On this trip you do exactly what you are told.' Zeina started to protest but was silenced by Shrapnel's raised hand and unusually stern expression. 'Exactly what you are told. Don't do anything else to draw attention to yourself. Do not let anyone see the aerocycle. For this trip, you are Jackson's quiet and boring guest from Ravenport, nothing more. Then, as soon as you make it back to the Willoughby Whale, you say you miss your dad and you want to go home. Promise me, Zeina! Promise me and I'll deliver the letter to your dad.'

CHAPTER 14

J ackson did his best not to scream as he pushed his breakfast around his plate. How had Zeina managed to get him into this mess? He was pleased to notice that she was also eating very little of the feast laid out before them. The dark shadows that ringed her eyes showed that she too had had very little sleep last night, but he supposed for her this was due to excitement rather than terror. He gulped down a little toast, his stomach doing somersaults every time he thought about getting back on an airship. The Willoughby Whale was so large that most of the time you forgot that you were flying at all. The thought of being surrounded again by all that sky, feeling every wobble and change in speed, made his heart race.

When they reached the platform, Jackson had to admit the *Raven* was the most impressive airship he had ever seen. It was much larger even than the *Golden Eagle*, the jewel of the Willoughby fleet, and unlike their airships, which were all painted the same shade of navy, the *Raven* was black with silvery stripes that stretched nose to tail. There was a crew loading supplies and ore into the hold. The first wisps of black smoke curling from the ship's funnels told Jackson that the engine room crew were already starting up the furnaces. Most alarming of all was the enormous harpoon gun fitted to the ship's bow.

'A relic left over from the good old days, she is,' said an old man carrying a crate of ore. He stopped next to the children where they were staring up, one in horror and the other in fascination, at the great silver blade. 'Back in the Second Age she was a whaling ship, of course. That blade has seen more blood and guts than any other!' Jackson began to feel hot and sweaty and was very glad of his mostly empty stomach. 'Course, we're not supposed to use them now,' the man continued sulkily. 'Now it's nothing but darts and nets. Although she does come in handy for seeing off any Smog Rats we come across. Still, I'd have liked to see a real whale hunt, just once. My father was a whaler, and his father before him. They used to make a mint out of their cuts of the blubber. My grandaddy once told me there was so much blood that—'

'Thank you, Joel!' Vivianne Steele raced down the gangway towards them. 'I'm sure Zeina and Jackson can't wait to hear every one of your stories, but that ore won't load itself, now, will it?'

'Right you are, Viv.' He picked up his crate and set off towards the hold. 'See you aboard, young 'uns!'

'Joel is harmless but just a little too fond of the olden days. Tells the most gruesome stories, most of which are completely fabricated, I would imagine. Are you all right there, Master Willoughby?' She put a reassuring hand upon his shoulder and squeezed. With her hair tied back by a green scarf and a pair of golden airship goggles resting on her head, she managed to look effortlessly glamorous despite the fact that she was wearing overalls. Her famous golden spyglass clanked at her belt.

'Yes,' he coughed, starting to feel ashamed of some of the things he had said the night before. 'I'm fine, thank you. Your ship is really impressive, Miss Steele.'

'Oh, you must call me Vivianne! We are going to be spending lots of time together and I know we will all become great friends. Now, if you leave your things here on the platform and follow me, my crew will load them into your rooms for you.'

Zeina hesitated before slipping off her backpack and placing it down next to Jackson's.

'Could I just ... bring mine with me?' she suggested tentatively.

'Oh, Zeina.' Vivianne's hands went to her cheeks. 'Don't tell me you've filled up your pack with a load of stolen silver and Jackson's grandma's jewellery?' She laughed, a lovely musical chuckle.

'No! NO! I haven't!'

And Zeina went so red that Jackson had to laugh too. She shot him a thunderous glare.

'Your things will be quite safe here, I can assure you,' Vivianne said, putting an arm around Zeina's shoulders. 'You don't want to be lugging them round while I give you the tour, that's all. Come on now, this way.' And she set off up the gangway to the main deck with Zeina and Jackson following behind.

'Isn't she glorious!' Vivianne stretched out both her arms and twirled around the deck. 'She was in a bit of a state when I first got her, but I've done her up, bit by bit, as the money came in.'

She linked arms with them both as they walked along the deck. The dreamy look on Zeina's face as she gazed up at her hero annoyed Jackson immensely. If it wasn't for her, he'd be travelling to Ravenport today – back just in time for some last-minute velocycle practice before the time trials.

'My rooms are at the stern and the rest of the crew have cabins below deck, all apart from Katu. He prefers it in the crow's nest.' She pointed towards a metal tower that stood taller even than the airship's funnels. At the very top Jackson could see a black-cloaked figure. 'It's better for tracking and navigation up there and keeps him and his moods out of the way of the rest of us. He'll keep us on course once we cross the Western Mountains and make sure we locate the whales' breeding ground in time.'

Jackson realised that despite it being his family's business, he actually had no idea how they were going to catch a sky whale, once they located one. A lump formed in his throat, remembering all those terrifying pictures he'd seen of monstrous wild whales, before their STAN system was fitted. He gulped; right now he just had to focus on taking off without throwing up. Steele was already pulling them up deck, towards the ship's bridge.

'We have four short-range airships on deck, used for scouting missions and picking up supplies mainly. Now, this, THIS is where the magic happens!' She danced into a large room of floor-to-ceiling windows. Levers, buttons and lights lined one wall and along the other was an untidy desk, covered in maps. Through the glass front, Jackson could see the harpoon gun, which seemed even more deadly up close. Below it, Vivianne's crew were as busy as worker bees, gathering supplies and bringing them back to their queen. Jackson tried to focus his eyes on the wooden slats of the floor, rather than the grey of the platform metres below them.

'This is where I captain the ship from!' Vivianne said, ruffling Zeina's head, which was pressed so hard against the glass that she left little smudgy nose marks behind. 'This is where I plot the route, check our progress and change our height or direction. We have short-range radio to communicate with the engine room and crow's nest. And a long-range radio – but that's for my use only.' She glared fiercely at them both for a second before grinning and plonking herself down in a high-backed chair. 'Just look at that view! You can imagine how fabulous it's going to be once we set off.'

Jackson felt the blood drain from his face. He shut his eyes as the room began to spin.

'I'd recognise that look anywhere, Jackson,' said Vivianne, grabbing his hand and patting it kindly. 'Airsickness is very common, you know. Even some of my own crew suffer from it at times. You'll be fine once we're up in the air, I promise.'

He looked into those emerald eyes, wanting to believe her more than anything, and felt his cheeks flush. A loud squawk made them all turn towards a golden cage where Albi hopped from one white foot to the other. Vivianne rushed over and scratched his head through the bars with one finger. She drew some biscuits from her pocket and fed him by hand.

'Is that a good idea?' Zeina asked. 'He nearly had Hamilton's finger off yesterday.'

'Oh, don't worry! Little Albi here is a sweetie, really.'

To Jackson's surprise, the bird fluffed up his feathers and cooed gently at her.

While the crew finished their jobs, black smoke changing from wisps to billows, a crowd of guests gathered on the Whale's main deck to watch the famous *Raven* take off. Hamilton positioned himself at the front of the crowd and waved a spotted silk handkerchief dramatically.

'Take care, my dears! Take care and have a fabulous time!'

He made a great show of removing his monocle and dabbing at his eyes with the handkerchief as the propellers started up.

Vivianne barked orders from her chair, pressed buttons and pulled levers. The *Raven* lurched up and away from the platform, making Zeina squeal with excitement. Jackson forced himself to keep his eyes open, despite the swirling of his insides. He breathed in and out steadily, focusing on the great flipper of the Willoughby Whale rather than the miles of sky beneath them. The ship accelerated alongside the beast, eventually bringing them up close to its enormous eye. For a moment it looked like a great glass ball, the clouds and the *Raven* reflecting back at them from the murky pupil. Then it blinked – so quickly that you might have thought you'd imagined it, were you not paying close attention. Something about that blink unnerved Jackson. While they had been aboard, he had almost forgotten that the Willoughby Whale, his hotel, was built on a living thing. It was so huge and so still. They never felt a breath, heartbeat or belly-rumble the whole time they had been aboard. The eye refocused. Now it looked right at the *Raven* – right at him.

CHAPTER 15

Zeina had been feeling tired after a restless night going over Shrapnel's words and the promise she had made him, but all that was washed away as the *Raven* ascended. She gasped as a vast sky full of opportunity stretched out before her. The Upper Atmosphere thrummed with activity. Vivianne huffed and tutted as she tried to navigate around the many airships. Eventually, she pulled a large lever next to her captain's chair and wound out a winch with some speed. The airship's bow tilted up, away from the clouds, causing Zeina and Jackson to grab on to the desk.

'Sorry! Should have warned you!' She wound the winch back in and the floor began to flatten out again. 'You all right there, Jackson?'

He caught his breath and nodded, although his face definitely had a distinctive green tinge to it. Zeina tried to ignore the little voice in her head that reminded her he was only stuck here because of her.

'We'll travel at this height by day, away from the whales and tourist ships. We'll have to fly at cloud level during the night otherwise we'll be easy pickings for the Smog Rats.'

At the window's upper edge, the bright blueness bled into an inky dark. Miles below them, the dense cloud layer looked like mountains sculpted from thick whipped cream.

'Come and have a look at this.' Vivianne's arm scooped Zeina in closer. Zeina's heart felt like it had tripled in size. She leaned forward eagerly towards an ancient-looking map. The Eastern, Southern and Western Continents were printed in neat black, with illustrations showing the position of the Western Mountains and the Southern Sea. The Northern Continent had been sketched on later, in what Zeina guessed was Vivianne's own hand. Dashed lines showed the quickest routes to each continent, and annotations warned of "high winds", "thunder-fog" or "Smog Rat territory".

'Here, across the Southern Sea, is the Southern Continent. Discovered right back in the First Age. Early airships avoided going west, due to wild sky whale attacks, and weren't able to fly far north, due to fuel consumption. Now, there's not much of anything that interests me in the south – it's mainly desert on the ground and its Upper Atmosphere is horrendously touristy. The southern cruising circuit is packed all year round, with rich Aboves endlessly sunbathing and popping to each other's whales for dinner parties,' she scoffed, rolling her eyes mischievously at Jackson.

'Next to be discovered was the Western Continent. By the Second Age, airships had developed harpoons, of course, so sky whales weren't as much of a problem. However, it wasn't until ten years ago, after lots of the wild whales were gone, that I went far enough west to discover the Forest of Howlingwood. That's where the Kotarth are from and where the remaining wild whales are most accessible for capture. It will be our final destination. Once we cross the Western Mountains and navigate the mining grounds, Katu can guide us to the nearest wild whale.'

Jackson gulped. 'What if the whale attacks us first?' he asked tentatively.

'Don't worry, Jackson. This must be at least our fiftieth sky whale capture and I've never had one of my crew injured in any way. We're professionals. That's right, isn't it, Katu?'

Zeina hadn't noticed the solemn figure of the navigator enter the bridge. His long dark robes hung in folds and a sleek silver dagger shone at his belt. With his hood down, Zeina could make out the bronze markings that dappled his cheeks, forehead and ear tips. At the end of his short snout was a small triangle of black nose, and around his curved lips and whiskers were tufts of white fur that formed a beard. His huge golden eyes regarded her with an unmistakeable suspicion, his pupils the shape of black crescent moons.

'That's right, Miss Steele. There have been no human casualties in any of our many sky whale hunt missions.'

Zeina was sure the tip of his pink tongue licked his jagged canines as he said the word "human".

'How do we capture the whale once we find one?' Zeina directed her question to Vivianne, keeping her back firmly turned on Katu. Now the excitement of take-off was subsiding, Shrapnel's warning echoed in her mind. The rest of Steele's crew seemed friendly enough, but she certainly didn't trust *him*.

'We've got a fail-proof system, using the short-range airships and a specially made steel net,' said Vivianne proudly. 'We use darts only when we have to and haven't *once* needed the harpoon. Keeping the whale as calm as possible until we get it back to the STANS facility is the objective – safest for both us and the whale. We need it in top condition before handing it over to the investors. In this case, that's you and your lovely uncle, Jackson!'

Jackson shuffled his feet uncomfortably.

'It's only quite recently that airships have been adapted to carry enough ore to go as far as the Northern Continent,' Vivianne continued, pointing to the map. 'The *Raven* was the first. When I stepped down on to the ice, I couldn't believe how beautiful and desolate it was, nothing but white for miles and miles. And then there were the Palik Caves and meeting the Ice Bears – and all the treasure, of course.' Her eyes gleamed. 'Who knows what we will discover in the future, just so long as the ore keeps coming – and the money, of course! That's where your lovely lot come in, Jackson!'

She gave him a friendly nudge.

'We'll head north before looping round to the west. The Northern Outpost of Wren is the best place to stock up with fuel and supplies before crossing the Western Mountains, so that's where we're heading first. Should be there in time for lunch.' She pointed to a tiny dot surrounded by jagged mountains on the border of the Northern Continent. 'If you're both feeling up to it, I'd go out on deck for a bit now. This will probably be the only time you'll ever get to see the whale cruising lane from above. We'll be off the beaten track after Wren.'

Zeina and Jackson went out on the deck, an uneasy silence filling the space between them. Zeina sat upon the decking at the stern, dangling her legs through the railings and out into the wind. From here she spotted at least five whale hotels, so far below them now that they looked like nothing but minnows in a vast ocean. The shifting cloud layer was ragged and wispy in parts, meaning they got brief snapshots of the continent below. There was nothing but grey smog-filled cities to start with, but as they proceeded north, cities changed into hilltop villages with animals grazing on the slopes and crops growing in the valleys. The land became progressively steep and rocky until, finally, the only thing to be seen was snow-capped mountaintops.

'Zeina! Jackson!' Vivianne's voice sang from the bridge. 'Time to get dressed up!'

Vivianne was waiting for them with thick furry coats – a cream one for Zeina that mimicked Vivianne's own, and a big shaggy brown one for Jackson. They were enormous on them but snug and warm, something they were extremely glad of as the *Raven* made its way down into a valley surrounded by white craggy mountains. Zeina was mesmerised by the tiny flakes of ice that descended from the sky in a dainty dance. This must be snow; she had read about it in a book she'd found at the scrapyard. Delighted, she turned her face upwards, sticking out her tongue to catch them.

Vivianne laughed. 'I suppose this is the first time either of you have seen real snow, eh? The smog ruins it for us on the Eastern Continent.'

'Isn't there any smog here at all? We don't need our respirators on the ground?' Jackson asked, watching enthralled as the delicate flakes melted in the palm of his hand.

'Sometimes, but only when there's a strong wind from the south,' Her nose took in a deep long breath. 'This smells like good, clean northern air to me!'

The mountains took Zeina's breath away – steep summits like the teeth of a giant beast piercing the sky. Although Wren itself was simply a small collection of snow-covered buildings, the awesome scenery surrounding it made it feel magical.

✳

After a quick stop at Wren for the crew of the *Raven* to load up the ship with crates from a warehouse, it was time to set off once more. They waved from the deck as the airship rose slowly out of the valley and above the clouds again. Zeina noticed that Jackson was nowhere near as nervous this time – less sweaty and his face certainly wasn't as green. As they walked back to the bridge to join Vivianne, she thought about their fight; neither of them had spoken to the other since.

There were some things she wanted to say – not to apologise for the trip, obviously, as it was already turning out to be an amazing experience for them both – but maybe that she *was* sorry about the time trials. She wanted him to apologise for all those awful things he had said about her and Vivianne first but wasn't sure how to make that happen.

Reaching the bridge, these thoughts were put completely out of her head by the sight of Vivianne, Katu and another crewman, their heads together and their voices low, examining a long golden tube. It looked like . . . her aerocycle!

'Hey!' She rushed towards them, grabbing the aerocycle roughly from the crewman's hands. 'That's mine!'

'It's all right, Zeina.' Vivianne tried to put her arm around Zeina but she retreated, arms hugging the aerocycle to her chest. She *knew* she shouldn't have left her backpack like that.

'It's mine! He's been through my stuff.' She pointed angrily at Katu, who snarled back at her.

'It's all right, Zeina,' Vivianne repeated, her voice serene. 'It wasn't Katu. Boris here was taking your things to your cabin when your pack fell open and this thing, this – aerocycle, did you call it? Well, it fell out on to the floor and he didn't know what it was, so he brought it to me.'

Zeina's arms relaxed a little but she still scowled suspiciously at Katu. Not fastening her backpack properly did sound like something she'd do. However, she was almost certain this morning she had made sure it had been all zipped up, especially after Shrapnel's warning.

'I can assure you Boris has no interest in stealing anything. Do you, Boris?'

'No, Viv.'

'In fact, we treat theft very seriously on the *Raven*. Anyone found stealing is discharged from duty immediately and handed over to the lawkeepers. It's too much of a risk. First theft, then disorder and mutiny, and I won't have that on my ship.'

'Treated very seriously, it is,' Boris echoed.

'Now, my crew are always on the lookout for Smog Rat spies.' Vivianne's voice became low and serious. 'They're under strict instructions to report anything unusual to me. That's all this is, I promise, and if you can explain what this contraption is, then it will be released back to you straight away. Go on now, Katu, Boris – off you go,' she added firmly. 'I think Zeina, Jackson and I can take it from here.'

Katu's eyes scanned greedily over the aerocycle in Zeina's arms one last time before he left.

'Come now, please, Zeina,' Vivianne asked kindly.

Zeina did not want to explain at all, but she didn't really have a choice. She reluctantly unfolded the golden tube until it clicked into place.

'Remarkable, but what is it? What does it do?' Vivianne beckoned to Zeina and hesitantly, she handed over her prized possession.

'It's an aerocycle. I invented it myself, using parts from a velocycle and parts from . . . an airship.' The last part wasn't technically a lie. 'It's a flying machine.'

'It flies?' Vivianne asked, her face contorted with disbelief. 'How? Where is the ore burnt?' She turned it over in her hands, examining every inch.

'Um, it doesn't need ore. You just—'

'What? No ore at all?'

Zeina shook her head.

'Really? Now, that's fascinating.' Vivianne twirled the pedals in wonder. 'How is it powered? You must give me a little demonstration during our trip. Tell me, have you ever flown it in the Upper Atmosphere?'

Zeina shook her head again, her insides battling between wanting to keep her promise to Shrapnel and wanting to impress the famous explorer.

'If this works, it is quite the invention, Zeina! No wonder your father wants you back as his apprentice. What a marvel!'

Zeina blushed with pride.

'Well, I can see no reason why you shouldn't have it back, just so long as you promise not to attempt to fly it alone – only with my supervision, OK? I'm responsible for your safety and I take that very seriously indeed.'

Zeina nodded and Vivianne carefully handed her back the aerocycle, her eyes sparkling with delight.

CHAPTER 16

During the first days of the trip, Jackson did his best to push away thoughts about the time trials. They would go ahead without him and there was nothing he could do. No matter how much this stung, the daily happenings aboard the *Raven* provided a welcome distraction.

Mornings were mainly spent out on deck, enjoying the fresh, cool air and gentle sunlight as the ship ascended from its night-time bed among the clouds. Vivianne had been right about his flight sickness – it got easier day by day.

By the time the midday sun was at its highest, the children were forced to retreat to the coolness of their cabins. On hearing that Zeina had no books of her own at home and Jackson only textbooks, Steele lent them her collection of stories written in the Second Age. These were nothing like anything Jackson had read before. They were tales of heroes and heroines, discoveries, battles with sky whales, dramatic failures and then finally a triumphant victory. He and Zeina had still not spoken of their fight – Jackson refused to be the one to bring it up – but together they would eat their lunches in quiet civility, surrounded by piles of books and maps. Zeina pored over the most gut-wrenching pictures, brushing away the crumbs that fell from her open mouth.

Once the sun began its descent, it was time for the children to venture back up into the afternoon light and do some work.

'Everyone on my ship works as equals,' Vivianne often said. 'Above or Below, adults or children, everyone mucks in.'

Zeina, of course, wanted to spend all her time on the bridge with Vivianne. She was a natural helmsman and quickly learned the controls needed to steer the ship. Steele allowed her to use her monocular spyglass and even trusted her to maintain and repair parts of her beloved airship, which left Jackson feeling useless at first.

Aboves were not generally taught "skills" but at least his geographical knowledge came in useful when it came to navigation – something that Zeina did not have the patience for. Vivianne showed him how to plan their route and make way for the unexpected, such as high winds or approaching storms. Up in the crow's nest, he and Katu would scrutinise their progress using compasses to check direction and spyglasses to spot landmarks. For once, Jackson was very glad that his tutor had forced him to read *The Geography of the Four Continents* from cover to cover. Katu's calm, quiet nature made Jackson feel calm too, but whenever flight sickness got the better of him he could retreat to the comfort of the engine room. Despite the gruelling work, the noise, the heat and the dust, to Jackson's surprise he enjoyed helping out. The rowdy engine crew joked and teased him in the way he imagined the members of the Ravenport Racers team did with each other.

Although it annoyed him that Zeina had not apologised, it was nice to see her happy for once. She seemed more considerate; less angry with everyone. Jackson could see how much she loved being with Vivianne, working alongside her, learning about the world from which she had been hidden for so long.

'Who needs an innovator when you've got Zeina Starborn, eh?' Vivianne said as Zeina tightened a loose winch or tinkered with the control panel. 'Smog Rats will be after you if we're not careful! Won't they, Katu?'

'Quite, Miss Steele,' replied Katu, tabby brows furrowed, tail swishing beneath his cloak. Zeina's dislike of the catty navigator was evidently quite mutual.

Every evening the crew ate together out on deck, under the stars. Dinner was a mismatch of smoked meats, salted fish, pickles and biscuits – nothing as grand as Jackson was used to but tasty all the same. As they ate, the crew would sing songs, tell stories and laugh loudly. This went on late into the evening, when gas lamps were needed to make out faces. Vivianne decided when it was time for bed for all but those on the night shift. The crew were a rowdy lot but always did exactly as she asked.

The airship continued its course by night but at a slower speed, half hidden in the uppermost layer of the clouds. Here Katu's crow's nest still had a clear view in case of any Smog Rat ambushes, but the *Raven*'s silvery stripes camouflaged it from sight.

On the afternoon of their third day, Vivianne treated her crew to a short diversion into the Lower Atmosphere to visit Ragrock Mountain, a famous landmark for airships travelling west. With the *Raven* anchored to a large rocky outcrop, the crew enjoyed a sunny afternoon feast out on deck. A beautiful glacial waterfall, the source of the River Wader, cascaded in the background. Jackson could not believe this clear water would eventually become the grey sludge that meandered through Ravenport to its mouth at the Eastern Sea.

When Vivianne called an end to the break, she led the way back to the bridge, then stopped dead in her tracks. 'What on EARTH are you doing!?' Her tone was tinged with a steely anger. Katu was crouched down fiddling with one of the dials as the long-range radio crackled and buzzed. 'That radio is for MY use and MY use alone – as you well know!'

This rule had been made only too clear to Jackson and Zeina; the radio was *solely* for Vivianne's use. It was too risky; used incorrectly it would give away their position to Smog Rat ships or spies. Katu's ears flattened and all the hair stood up on his neck. He had been so intent on the radio that he had not heard them approaching. He stepped away rather guiltily as Steele marched over, snatching the chrome mouthpiece away from him.

'I was just—' he started.

'I don't care what you were JUST doing, Katu. This is a serious danger to us all!'

'No, Miss Steele, let me explain, please.' His nose twitched and his whiskers bristled. 'I was examining the map for the next part of our route when a bulletin came through. It sounded important so I thought best to try and tune in as quickly as possible.'

'WELL?' she demanded. 'What was it, Katu?'

His cat-like eyes darted around the room, eyeing Zeina, Jackson and Vivianne nervously. 'It's a little sensitive, Miss Steele. If I could just—'

'You *may not*, Katu. I must know if we've been compromised *immediately*!'

It was then that the metal speaker in Vivianne's hand began to crackle to life. A voice came through – faint at first, but then louder and clearer.

'BUZZZ . . . SMOG RATS . . . BUZZZ.'

Vivianne dropped to her knees, turning the dial back and forth until the message came through.

'*GOLDEN EAGLE* CRASHED IN NORTHERN CONTINENT . . . SMOG RAT SHIP IMPLICATED . . . THIRTY-TWO CASUALTIES IDENTIFIED SO FAR . . . ALL OTHERS MISSING, PRESUMED DEAD . . . LORD AND LADY WILLOUGHBY AMONG THE DECEASED . . . SMOG RATS EVADED CAPTURE . . . ALL AIRSHIPS IN AREA MUST REMAIN VIGILANT . . . REPEAT . . . AIRSHIP CRASH IN NORTHERN—'

Jackson's head swam. He staggered backwards, colliding with the map table and knocking compasses and maps to the floor as the room began to swim. The buzzing faded and then stopped as Vivianne switched the radio off and in two long strides she was across the room, enveloping him in her arms.

CHAPTER 17

Early the next morning, Zeina was awoken by shouts and running footsteps. Bleary-eyed, she pulled on her overalls – she'd had very little sleep for worrying about Jackson.

He hadn't said a word since he'd heard about his parents on the radio. After that awful message, Steele had guided him to his cabin and talked to him with the door closed. Later, when Zeina took him in some dinner on a tray, she saw that he was huddled up on his bunk, face to the wall, asleep or at least pretending to be.

Knocking gently on his cabin door, she opened it tentatively, only to find him already missing from his bed, the food from last night untouched. She found Jackson out on deck, still in pyjamas but wrapped in one of the fur coats Vivianne had lent them. Glassy-eyed, he watched the crew rushing about and shouting at each other, some carrying long wooden poles. The *Raven* was encased in a mist so thick that

Zeina could make out very little of their surroundings. In an effort to see more clearly, she went over to the port-side railings, causing Jackson to leap into life, grabbing her arm and pulling her back.

'Don't,' he mumbled numbly.

'Why? Where are we?'

'Just watch. You'll see.'

Zeina didn't have to wait for long. Out of the mist and only a few centimetres from the railings where she had been heading, a great wall of rock emerged. It was so close that she could make out the tiny plants clinging to the cliff face. There was an outburst of shouts from the crew and a flurry of activity. Men rushed towards the port-side railings with their poles and pushed against the rock face until it disappeared into the fog once again.

'What was that?'

'We're in the Western Mountains,' replied Jackson. 'But something tells me that we're lower than we should be.'

'Shouldn't you be resting?' Zeina asked him nervously, taking in his red-rimmed eyes.

'No,' he sniffed, tears pooling. 'I don't want to be alone. Rather be out here.'

'I'm so sorry, Jackson.' Zeina grabbed his hand in hers as her words began to tumble out. 'I'm sorry about everything, about your parents, about our fight. I should have said something before. I wanted to; I don't know why I didn't. I should have remembered about the time trials, about our deal. I'm so sorry.'

Jackson laughed, a sniffly grunt. 'None of that matters any more.' He used the cuff of his coat to wipe away tears. 'You know, I never really knew them. I never saw them. I don't know why I'm so upset.'

Zeina shuffled in closer, squeezing his hand. 'I never really knew my mum either – she died when I was very small. It doesn't stop you feeling sad about it. Whatever happens, they are still your parents.'

The ship's deck tilted up suddenly. Zeina and Jackson huddled together to stop themselves from toppling over. Cliffs loomed again, this time causing a terrifying scrape down the starboard side. The crew rushed over with their poles, just in time to stop the ship's hull being broken to pieces. A loud crash from the stern made Zeina turn. The top of one of the funnels had collided with a rocky outcrop.

'Zeina, get down!'

Jackson pulled her to the floor, covering her head just seconds before a torrent of rock shards hit the deck. The ship lurched upwards again and Zeina gripped a nearby railing, desperately hanging on to Jackson to stop him from sliding backwards. There was another deafening scrape of stone on steel, a rumble and then crashes as more rocks struck the deck around them.

As the ship ascended, frequent rockfalls sent the crew scattering for cover. The fog grew thinner and the mountainsides on both port and starboard came into view. By the time Zeina felt safe enough to raise her head, the rocky cliff edges had been replaced by pointed mountain tops. The *Raven* evened out and the crew fell in an exhausted heap on the deck.

'Who was on the night shift?' Vivianne stormed out from the bridge, her white fur coat wrapped over her pyjamas. There was no answer. For the first time since the children came aboard, every single person was silent. Even Albi, who could usually be heard croaking and flapping from his cage, was completely soundless.

'Who is responsible for this mess? Who was in charge of following the flight path last night?'

'It was I, Miss Steele.' Katu appeared next to the children, head bowed.

'You?' she scoffed. 'Our *expert* navigator?'

'I'm sorry, Miss Steele. I must have fallen asleep.'

'On duty?!' Her eyes narrowed; her nostrils flared. If looks could kill, Zeina felt sure Katu would have been burnt alive on the spot, yet he seemed as calm and collected as always.

'Yes. I must apologise. At around oh-four-hundred hours. I awoke to find us lower than expected and then, of course, alerted the crew immediately.'

Vivianne glared at Katu and he stared back. Something that Zeina couldn't quite catch passed between them. Her heart fluttered in her throat – maybe Steele would fire him.

'It's a credit to this crew that we weren't all killed,' Vivianne growled. 'Have there been any sightings of Smog Rats in the area, Boris?'

'Not this morning, Vivianne.'

'We'll just have to hope we haven't been spotted then, won't we, Katu?' she continued through gritted teeth. 'You're off night shifts and I want you to stay in the engine room for the rest of the day. Joel will take your place in the crow's nest.' Her green eyes glinted. 'But first, go and clean out Albi's cage. With all the excitement this morning, he's made quite a mess. I'd go and find a pair of good, thick gloves before opening the door, if I were you.'

The crew broke their silence, sniggering and jeering, like a pack of dogs around its leader.

'As you wish, Miss Steele, and I do again most wholeheartedly apologise.' He bowed low and retreated.

'Well, back to work, everyone. We'll be over the mining grounds before you know it. Zeina, down to the bridge with me. Jackson, you head back to your cabin.'

'If it's all right, Vivianne, I'll go to the engine room. I'd rather be busy, I think.'

She smiled. 'There's a lad! It'll be all hands to the pump if we're to make up the time we've lost.'

That morning the crew worked harder than ever. Vivianne was in a foul mood, spending most of her time shouting demands. Despite this, Zeina loved every second. She felt important – a vital part of Steele's team. Working alongside Vivianne filled a little hole deep inside Zeina, replacing something that she hadn't even known was missing until then. It helped her brush away the guilt she felt about leaving her dad. She wondered what he would be doing now. Had Shrapnel handed over her letter? Did he know about Lord and Lady Willoughby? Ravenport would be packed after the news broke. She wondered how he would be managing all those airships without her.

Eventually they gained enough height that they were back just above the cloud layer, where only the very tops of the tallest mountains peeked through. Vivianne sighed and sat back in her chair.

'Finally, we're back on course. Zeina, go and tell everyone in the engine room to ease off a bit before we end up in the stars. Get Jackson for me and then go down to the galley to ask them to get lunch ready – extra portions for everyone after the work we've done this morning.'

By the time Zeina made it back up to the bridge, Jackson and Steele were talking together in low voices, Steele's hand upon Jackson's shoulder. Zeina shrank back, not wanting to intrude.

'Come on in, Zeina. Jackson and I have been discussing whether to continue the trip or, considering the recent news, return to Ravenport.'

Zeina's heart felt heavy all of a sudden. It was not her place to tell Jackson what to do, particularly considering all he had been through, but she couldn't go back now – not when she was so close to seeing a wild sky whale.

'He's decided that, for now, considering the fact that there are reports of Smog Rats in the north-east, we should continue. That's right, isn't it, Jackson?'

Jackson nodded, his eyes swimming. 'I don't want to go back to Ravenport just now.' His voice was wobbly, barely audible.

'No, lad.' Steele gave his shoulder a squeeze. 'It'll be chaos. Best to let the dust settle, eh?'

He nodded again.

'Right! It's time for something to take our minds off everything!' She linked arms with each of them and marched them out on to the deck. It was almost midday but the cool air over the mountains meant that the crew were sitting out, picking greedily at an early lunch and basking in the late-morning sun.

'Zeina, I've had the most amazing idea, just the thing to cheer us all up! I hope you won't mind, but I've sent Boris for your aerocycle. I think a little demonstration is just the thing to distract us all.'

Zeina's heart began to pound. This was going directly against what Shrapnel had made her promise. However, after Vivianne's mood that morning, what else could she do? She wasn't brave enough to disagree.

'Oh! I'm not even sure if it will fly up here.'

'Oh, tosh! That's not like you! Come on now, we're only five hundred metres or so above your platform in Ravenport – barely in the Upper Atmosphere at all! Where's that adventurous little Zee I've grown to love?'

Zeina's heart swelled, and so when Boris handed her the aerocycle she unfolded it, clicking everything into place surrounded by impressed ohhhhs and ahhhs from the watching crew. It seemed like many months had passed since she had ridden her aerocycle through her window and away from Willoughby Towers. Zeina had wanted to try the aerocycle out in the Upper Atmosphere, of course, but not like this, not in front of all these people. What if it didn't fly? Jackson looked as worried as she felt but, nevertheless, she got on, clicked the gear, just as she had done that first time, and began to pedal. To her great relief the aerocycle lurched upwards. She repositioned herself, turned the handlebars and

145

soared, leaving the deck and the mountaintops behind her. The crew erupted, Vivianne yelling loudly above them all.

'I knew you could do it, Zeina!'

Zeina beamed, pushing higher. She looped over the crow's nest and then weaved around the billows of smoke from the funnels. Vivianne beckoned her back down and swooped her up in a massive bear hug as she landed.

'That was fantastic, Zeina!' she grinned. 'But now I think it might be Jackson's turn?'

'No, no, no, no.' Jackson was shaking his head vigorously and turning a familiar greenish-white.

'Why not? You've shown on this trip that you can do anything, Jackson.' She put her arm around him. 'Plus a little birdy told me that you are quite the velocyclist.' Vivianne winked at Zeina. 'This is exactly the same – just up in the air. Come on.' She took the aerocycle from Zeina and helped Jackson on.

'I really don't think I . . .' he started, but was drowned out by the whole crew, who were now chanting, 'JackSON, JackSON, JackSON.'

Clicking the gear, he began to pedal. A terrified gasp came from him as he hovered about a metre from the deck. The aerocycle wobbled and for a second Zeina felt sure he would fall off. However, shoulders set in determination, he directed the handlebars upwards and pedalled steadily. Up, up, up he went – right over the crow's nest. Growing braver, he sped from bow to stern, travelling – to Zeina's dismay – at a much higher speed than she had managed. He returned to the deck to a cacophony of cheers. Vivianne went over to shake his hand and there was a lot of back-slapping and hair-ruffling from his friends in the engine room.

After last night, Zeina was relieved to feel some of the happiness she had felt over the last few days returning. From the sidelines she watched Jackson smiling and talking animatedly to the crew.

Katu appeared silently at her side.

'You shouldn't have shown her that.'

Zeina was instantly furious, happy thoughts gone. 'Oh, what do you know?'

'You'll see soon enough, I'm afraid,' he said, ears bristling.

'You're the one in trouble, not me. Your mistake could have killed us all. Why shouldn't I show her my aerocycle? It's an amazing invention and I was the very first person in the whole world to create one!'

He turned his head and his golden eyes bored straight into hers.

'You were? Really?' he asked, black-tipped lips smiling over dagger teeth, furry nose crinkled sceptically. There was a deep graze to his left brow, where red blood clotted with his dappled fur and an angry pink scar across the black of his nostrils – injuries from getting too close to Albi while cleaning the cage, Zeina supposed. It was like Katu somehow knew about the part she had stolen from her dad.

'You are quite like her, you know,' he said. 'How much so, I guess we will find out very soon.'

And with a swish of his tail, he slinked off below deck.

CHAPTER 18

'Zeina,' Jackson groaned, as she dragged his bed covers from his head. 'It's the middle of the night!'

'It's ten thirty, lazy bones. Come on!'

She held up a lantern, smiling at him just a little too close to his face. She'd been like this ever since he'd heard about his parents and, although glad of the distraction, her constant attention sometimes made him feel uncomfortable.

He was still trying to work out how he felt about everything. Pangs of misery gripped him whenever he thought about his parents, but there was also a feeling of sheer terror. He was now head of the Willoughbys, in charge of the fleet, the staff, the Willoughby Whale. He wanted to throw up every time he thought about it.

'It's so dark.' He rubbed his eyes, frowning at his porthole window. Usually they woke to clear views of blue sky but today there was nothing but thick, black smog.

'Viv wants you up on deck.' Zeina hassled him up to the

bridge, where he was relieved to find Vivianne in high spirits.

'Respirators!' she shouted, muffled by her own, which was held in place by a thick leather strap. 'Quickly! This stuff is toxic. Welcome, my dears, to the Western Mining Grounds!'

This smog was much worse than Ravenport's even on a bad day. It caught at the back of your throat, making you gasp and choke. Jackson was relieved when he could fill his lungs with deep, clean breaths, yet it felt strange to have a respirator strapped to his face once again. Thankfully, Vivianne also passed them both some goggles, as the fumes were beginning to burn at his eyes, making them sting with tears.

'Was this on our planned route?' asked Zeina, frowning as she examined the navigation map.

'No,' Vivianne said. 'I received a radio transmission from one of the guards down here – a message he wanted to pass on in person instead of risking interception. It wasn't too much of a detour and I thought you guys might like to see the mining grounds for yourselves. Shall we go in for a closer look?'

Zeina nodded and they both held on tightly while Vivianne wound in the winch.

Pointed brick smokestacks emerged, each emitting a swirling column of dark smog. Vivianne squinted, guiding the ship carefully between the giant towers of smoke.

By pressing their goggled faces right up against the window, the children could make out where great craters had been blown into the black earth below. Lines of men and women appeared and disappeared from tunnels around the craters' edges, each pushing a huge iron cart. Empty carts went in and carts laden with ore came out. They were pushed along a network of tracks, towards a conveyor of cranes, machinery and furnaces, where the air flickered in waves from the extreme heat. Ash rained down like dirty grey snow and everything, including the workers, was coated in a layer of fine black dust.

'Come on then, Master Willoughby.' Vivianne nudged him playfully. 'Show off that Above education of yours. Who discovered the Western Mining Grounds?'

Jackson appreciated that Vivianne still teased him, that she was treating him normally.

'Well, when ore from the Eastern Continent started to run out, the Chief Lawmaker set up a competition – a race for all explorers to go and find new mining grounds. There was a huge reward offered to the first to find new land with ore supplies and the person who won was—'

'Me!' Vivianne's face was mostly hidden by her respirator but Jackson could still tell she was grinning proudly.

Jackson noticed that Zeina was silent, her face still pressed intently against the window. Now they had drifted a little closer to the mine, more of the people working there became visible. Instead of respirators and goggles, the workers all wore masks that covered the entirety of their faces. Each mask had a round mouthpiece that stuck out like a snout dotted with holes, and two large, dark eyes on either side, making them look more like strange, other-worldly monsters than human beings. Their overalls covered their heads in tight hoods, and rubbery gloves came right up to their elbows. What surprised Jackson was that some of the smaller busy figures must have only been about his age.

'I've never met anyone who worked in the mining grounds,' said Zeina without removing her face from the window. 'Who are all these people?'

'Mostly criminals, my love,' answered Vivianne. 'Let's face it, you wouldn't work here unless you had to.'

Zeina frowned.

'She doesn't believe me! Go on, Jackson, you tell her.'

He hesitated. 'Yeah . . . that's right. Once the mines got going, the lawmakers closed the prisons and started sending criminals out here to work their sentences instead.' Jackson had always known this but had never really thought about it until now. Faced with the reality, it seemed kind of wrong.

'They get much better food than they ever did in prison,' Vivianne said coolly. 'And if they work really hard, they can get their sentences reduced or even a job onboard an airship.

I've taken on a couple of crewmembers after they finished mining sentences. Besides, we need this ore mined one way or another.'

Zeina continued to stare sadly at the little masked figures. Jackson wasn't totally convinced either – if Vivianne thought it was best for everyone, he was *almost* certain it was a good idea. Surely lawkeepers wouldn't send any old person out here into this awful toxic wasteland? But what could those small ones have done that was so bad they deserved this?

A small two-man airship drew up alongside the *Raven*. Its overalled occupants shouted through their respirators in order to be heard above the clamour of the machinery below.

'MISS STEELE! WHAT AN HONOUR! THANK YOU FOR COMING.'

'THAT'S ALL RIGHT, SMITH,' Vivianne cupped her hand around her respirator and yelled back. 'WHAT DID YOU NEED TO TELL ME?'

'YESTERDAY WE RECEIVED REPORTS OF AN UNREGISTERED SHIP OVER THE MOUNTAINS.'

'SMOG RATS?'

'VERY LIKELY. BUT NOT THE *NIGHTJAR*. A SMALLER SCOUTING SHIP. WE LOST IT IN THE SMOG, SO WE BLASTED SOME NEW ORE DEPOSITS – IT HAD THE DESIRED EFFECT: THUNDER-FOG STORM – A BAD ONE.'

Jackson gasped. He'd heard about thunder-fog. A terrible side effect from the high smog and fumes let off by the mining grounds was that the air could become flammable. Sometimes blasts could set off a storm, great purple clouds of thunder and lightning that no ship could escape until it burnt itself out. He'd never heard of anyone starting one purposely until now.

'WE INTERCEPTED A MAYDAY CALL – THE SHIP HAS CERTAINLY CRASHED SOMEWHERE. MIGHT BE THE CREW ABOARD KNOW WHERE TO FIND THE INNOVATOR.'

'WE NEED TO FIND THAT SHIP BEFORE THE *NIGHTJAR* DOES!'

'CERTAINLY, MISS STEELE. WE HAVE EVERY AVAILABLE SHIP OUT LOOKING FOR THEM AND WILL KEEP A CLOSE EAR ON THE RADIO FOR ANY MORE MAYDAY CALLS.'

'I CAN ALWAYS COUNT ON YOU, SMITH!'

Vivianne directed the *Raven* up. Smith, his airship and the smokestacks all disappeared into the thick fumes.

'So what do you two make of that then?' Vivianne's eyes were alight with excitement.

'I don't understand,' Zeina replied, looking as confused as Jackson felt. 'Did they *make* the ship crash? Why do they want to find this Innovator so much?'

'The Smog Rats are not only dangerous but selfish, Zeina. Their Innovator has designed new technology that could change our world for the better, but instead of sharing it, they use it to attack and thieve.'

Zeina seemed satisfied by this explanation. However, remembering the pictures he had seen of thunder-fog during his studies and thinking about those masked figures fetching ore for the crates, Jackson wasn't so sure.

CHAPTER 19

I t felt to Zeina as if their journey over the Western Mining Grounds would never end, that they would be lost in a world of smog for ever, but finally the *Raven* cut through the last of the clouds and into a new world altogether. Zeina and Jackson had escaped to the crow's nest in the hope it might be a little cooler up there and sat with their legs dangling over the side. Katu stood behind, spyglass in hand. Since crossing the mountains, he had spent even more time than usual alone in the crow's nest, tracking whales.

The short-range radio crackled to life.

'Katu, update.' Vivianne's voice was curt and impatient.

'Just a few more miles, Miss Steele,' Katu replied.

The smog became thinner until there was none left at all, just clouds, puffed and white, floating some way above them. The children released themselves from their masks and goggles, breathing in the clean air and blinking in the afternoon sun. This new world was one of trees – trees that

Zeina had never seen anything like before. They were each as tall as Willoughby Towers and very thin, with pointed needle tops. They grew densely, spiked and woven around each other, their branches competing for light, sticking out at angles like the bristles of a brush.

'The Forest of Howlingwood,' breathed Zeina. This was certainly more like what she had imagined the Western Continent to be. Her heart leapt – she was so close to seeing a sky whale!

Katu scoffed. 'Howlingwood,' he muttered.

'Isn't this where the Kotarth are from, Katu?' Jackson asked.

'This is my home, yes. But do we call this forest Howlingwood? No.'

'Sorry,' Jackson apologised, quickly turning to Zeina. 'That's just what Vivianne named it when she first came here. When the wind blows through the forest, the branches make a sound like a human howling in despair—'

'Sounds like a pretty good name to me then,' Zeina interrupted.

Katu looked down at her with disdain.

'To *you* it may sound like howling but to *us* it does not,' he hissed. 'The different noises the trees make is a form of communication, a way that the forest warns us of danger or signals that something is coming. It was successful in keeping humans away for many years. That was until Miss Steele arrived.'

'Well, she's brave. That's why,' Zeina hissed, and although Katu's expression did not change, the fur began to stand up on the back of his neck.

'Uh . . . how long do you think it will be until we see some whales, Katu?' Jackson changed the subject quickly.

'Not long, Master Willoughby. The pod I have been tracking are nearby. I can feel it.'

'Pod?' Zeina asked. She was beginning to wonder how exactly they were going to catch the whale. A pod suggested more than one wild whale, which sounded dangerous.

'Yes, Miss Starborn.' Katu smiled sarcastically, whiskers bristling. 'Sky whales travel in family pods. Did you not know that? They come here at this time of year to breed and show their young ones where they are from.'

'Oh.' Zeina stared up at him, curiosity battling against her hatred of him. When she had imagined capturing a wild sky whale, she thought of the old newspaper articles from the First Age, drawings of whales with teeth bared crashing through ancient airships, heroines battling against vicious beasts to save the day.

'Yes. And we must find them soon,' Katu continued. 'Due to the extent of the mining grounds, their visits to this spot are now limited. Wild sky whale pods used to visit us here for months at a time but now spend most of their year above the limit of the Upper Atmosphere, which is a great shame.'

'Aren't the Kotarth scared when they visit? What about attacks?' Jackson asked.

Zeina understood that even young sky whales were dangerous. She remembered once finding a newspaper article from the Second Age about the Attack of the *Goshawk*. The passenger ship had been ambushed by two adolescent males who had made a game out of batting the ship between them like a ball. Eventually one of them bit the ship right in two and not a single person aboard survived.

Katu scoffed again.

'No, Master Willoughby, the Kotarth are not afraid of sky whales. We have a great respect for them, as they do for us. We do not venture into their airspace, just as they do not swoop down into our forest and pluck us from our trees. There has *never* been an attack on the Kotarth, not in the millennia that they have come here. It's *humans* they attack – those that pollute their home and steal their family members for their floating hotels.'

Jackson flushed, head bowed. He seemed almost to shrink down to half his normal size.

'If you love them so much, then why do you help Vivianne track them?' Zeina retaliated.

'We are not all free to choose our own path, Miss Starborn. Some of us have our futures decided for us. I should think *you* understand that well enough.'

Before Zeina could respond, Katu's ears pricked up suddenly and his whiskers twitched. 'There,' he purred, lifting the spyglass to his eye. 'In the distance.'

Zeina and Jackson followed the direction of the spyglass. At first they could see nothing. Then distant grey blurs came into focus. Soon they could make out V-shaped tails and rounded fins, and then flippers and upturned mouths with rows of white teeth. The larger whales flew slowly, gracefully, gliding between the carpet of the forest and the cloud layer above. The smaller, younger whales darted between the adults, swooping up into the clouds and then nosediving back down. Sometimes they tumbled and turned about each other, playing some sort of game, before racing to catch up with the adults again. Unlike the Willoughby Whale, these whales all had striped markings along their backs and at the edges of their tail flukes and flippers. Each whale's markings were unique – different shapes and colours – and to Zeina's great surprise, the markings seemed to glow. They became brighter and duller as the whales flew. The adults' markings changed so gradually that you could barely tell it was happening, but the markings of the smaller whales faded and flashed quickly as they darted and played.

Zeina was captivated. She had pushed her face between the bars of the railing and saw that Jackson had stood up to lean right over, his mouth open and any fear of heights quite forgotten.

'What are those glowing stripes?' he asked. 'I've never seen anything like them before.'

'Those are called lumina lines,' Katu replied quietly. 'Wild sky whales use them to communicate with each other. Once a whale is away from its pod for a time, the lumina lines fade. Whales fitted with the STAN system cannot communicate with other whales and so the lines disappear altogether—'

Katu's sombre voice was interrupted by a shout from the deck below.

'Zeina! Jackson! Are you up there?' It was Vivianne. She spotted them and waved, smiling widely. 'Come down here, my loves! We have a lot of work to do!'

As she and Jackson descended the ladder, something wrestled inside Zeina. If this was the moment she had been waiting for, why did she have this strange twisting in her belly?

The deck was a hive of activity. Crewmembers ran this way and that, shouting to each other and carrying ropes and nets. Joel was in the centre, sweating as he turned a winch, which unfolded a great iron crane. An enormous hook clanked from the crane's arm. Three of the short-range airships were being manned and prepared for take-off. A pilot clambered into each cockpit, while another of the crew was helped into a harness attached to the airship's bow. They were strapped upright, facing forwards, and each carried a large dart gun. Whenever darts had been mentioned before, Zeina had pictured something that would simply sedate the whale, but these looked more like smaller versions of the *Raven*'s harpoon. Each dart was razor-sharp and had a long metal chain that attached to the ship's bow.

The fourth short-range airship was already in the air. It had flown over to the starboard side and was clipping a giant steel net to the hook of the crane.

Suddenly, there was an eerie howl from the forest below. The trees bristled and swayed in the wind and it sounded as though there were a hundred people screaming in agony from their branches.

'This way.' Vivianne grabbed them both. 'No time to dawdle! We have to get going before they realise we're here.'

The ship was ascending towards the cloud layer.

'The dartmen are asking which one you want, Viv?' Boris had arrived from the deck, a little breathless and flustered.

'Oh, let's ask our benefactor, shall we?' She smiled. 'Go on then, Master Willoughby. Which one do you want?'

'Which one?' Jackson asked, startled.

'Yes, which one? Quickly! Choose before we reach the cloud layer.' She waited for a response that did not come and then became impatient. 'What's the matter?' Boris was now hopping from foot to foot, flustering around Steele impatiently. 'Fine, I'll choose. We'll have the young male with the greyish-purple lumina lines, please, Boris.' She pointed to one of the smaller whales racing alongside his mother. 'He looks small enough to take but big enough to survive the journey back.'

'No,' Jackson yelled. 'I don't want it. I don't want any of them!'

And to Zeina's surprise, relief flooded her body. She went to Jackson's side, grabbing his hand in support as Vivianne turned to them, incredulous.

'Whatever is the matter with you two?'

'We can't take it,' Zeina gulped. 'It's a baby – it's not right.' Tears began to prick at her eyes but she blinked them away. She didn't want to cry in front of Vivianne.

'*Baby*? What are you talking about? It's a whale, not a baby. Would you prefer an adult one?' Vivianne laughed and the crewmembers rushing around her bayed and chuckled. 'Even the *Raven* can't tackle a fully grown whale, my love.' Steele went to brush a stray curl of hair behind Zeina's ear but she backed away. Vivianne frowned. 'You've been talking to Katu, haven't you? Don't let him upset you, my darlings. The Kotarth are so sentimental about their beloved sky whales, but don't be fooled. Every single one of those young ones has the potential to become a fully grown airship destroyer by

163

next season. We're saving human lives by doing this. Not to mention the healthy profit it brings in for me and the Willoughby family, eh, Jackson?' He did not return her smile.

'Come now, Zeina. *You* must be excited? You've waited all your life to see a wild sky whale hunt.'

Zeina did not smile either; in fact, she couldn't look Vivianne in the eye.

'Oh, for goodness' sake!' Vivianne threw both arms up in the air. 'We haven't got time for this. Jackson, it doesn't matter what you think. Hamilton commissioned the hunt. It's already arranged and paid for. Crew, prepare yourselves.'

'No!' Zeina and Jackson shouted.

Steele looked furious and hurt. 'I would *remind* you that I am in charge here. Any more from either of you and you'll be sent to your cabins.'

The *Raven* burst through the cloud layer and hovered, the howling from the forest below muffled slightly by the clouds. The short-range ships got into formation, their harnessed crew leaning forward with dart guns at the ready. Every few minutes or so the hump of a young sky whale's back would come through the top layer of clouds. Then a tail, followed by their tail fins as they nosedived back down to the pod. There were greyish-blue lamina lines, brownish-green, dark blue-black.

'Wait, steady,' Vivianne commanded. 'The one we want is sure to break soon.'

The thought of one of those darts piercing the baby's hide made Zeina feel sick.

There was a stripe of purple and a sudden flurry of activity. Vivianne shouted and all three ships fired their dart guns.

'No!' yelled Zeina, not wanting to see but unable to look away.

Two of the darts missed, but the last was on target. The dart struck the whale's back, making it jolt in pain. The pilot and dartman of the ship cheered loudly. Zeina felt angry tears on her cheeks.

'Up now!' Vivianne yelled. 'No time to celebrate. You two,' she pointed sharply at the two ships that had missed, 'get down there in case we get any trouble from the pod.'

The ship attached to the winning dart flew upwards with great speed, dragging the baby, tail first, above the clouds. The sky whale made desperate attempts to fly down towards its pod. Confused and terrified, its lumina lines flashed frantically. Below the clouds Zeina heard the sound of more darts being fired and a low, urgent moaning from the rest of the pod.

'Quick! Drive it into the net before the adults surface!'

Then it was the fourth airship's turn to leap into action. One end of the metal net was bolted to its bow, the other end held in place by the crane's hook. As the dartship flew up and round, dragging the baby whale with it, this ship circled the whale. It drew the net around the struggling animal and then flew back to the crane arm, unhooking the net from itself and drawing it in towards the crane. Joel turned the winch, trapping the whale completely. The crane swung violently and the whale hung over the deck, struggling and flashing and making a low moaning sound.

'Let it go!' Jackson shouted, grabbing Steele's arm. Zeina was frozen to the spot, forced to watch the awful spectacle and powerless to stop it.

'I'll wring the neck of that Kotarth!' Vivianne shook Jackson off violently. 'Getting you all wound up like this.'

How could Steele have done this fifty times before and come back to do it again? How could her hero be OK with this? Zeina leapt into action, grabbing Vivianne's arm and pulling at her too.

'No! Let it go now!' Zeina pleaded desperately.

'There's no time for this!' Vivianne exploded. 'Boris, Jamison, hold Jackson and Zeina until we get away. We could be struck by an adult at any time. Ready the harpoon! They won't follow us past the—'

There was a sudden loud crash and the *Raven* lurched sideways. Crew toppled over; maps went flying. Zeina fell, striking her head on the edge of the navigation desk and then all went black.

CHAPTER 20

Zeina's eyes fluttered open and Jackson breathed a sigh of relief.

'Zeina? Can you hear me?'

She blinked and tried to sit up. Reaching up to her temple to feel the bandage that was there, she groaned and sank back down to the floor.

'Don't get up! You banged your head. Been out for a few hours,' Jackson explained, replacing a blanket around her shoulders.

'What? Who?' Zeina asked, wincing in pain as she gestured towards her bandaged head.

'Katu did that,' Jackson said quietly. 'He carried you down to your cabin once the whale stopped chasing us and then cleaned and bandaged you up. Joel wanted to put some stitches in with a sewing needle like "the good old days" but Katu wouldn't let him.'

'We're . . . back over the mining grounds, aren't we?' Zeina

167

squinted, sniffing the air, which was once again tinted with an oily stench.

'Yeah. They turned around straight away to shake the adult whale off – she said it wouldn't follow us back into the smog.'

The mention of the whale seemed to flip a switch in Zeina's head. She sat bolt upright, ignoring Jackson's pleas to stay still.

'The whale! We have to do something!'

'I tried, Zeina.' He looked away, ashamed. 'I told her to let it go. I told her I didn't want it. She said she worked for Hamilton, not for me, and that I'd change my mind when I got home, that it was all Katu's fault for getting in my head. I shouted at her, at all of them, but they just laughed. Katu said there was nothing that would change her mind.'

'Katu? What does he know!' Zeina spat. 'This is all his fault! He tracked the pod for her.'

'I don't think he had a choice, Zeina.'

Zeina scoffed, 'Of course he had a choice! I never trusted him.'

'You're wrong,' Jackson replied. 'I think he's been working against Steele for a while, that he's been trying to slow everything down. Don't you think it was weird that he just happened to be near the radio when that message came through about my parents? And then he's supposed to be this expert navigator but manages to send us way off course in the mountains? It's like he has to help her but he doesn't want to, like she's forcing him somehow.'

Katu hadn't actually said any of this to Jackson but he had watched Katu as he bandaged up Zeina with care, his crescent eyes wide and sad. He looked how Jackson felt – ashamed.

Zeina tried to stand, leaning on Jackson's shoulder to stop herself from keeling over. She brushed off his appeals for her to get back into bed.

'We are going to sort this out now. I know that if I talk to Vivianne, she'll see sense. Maybe it's *her* being forced?' Zeina's eyes flickered with hope. 'She wouldn't do that to the whale unless she had to, I know she wouldn't.'

Jackson was almost certain that Zeina would not be able to change Vivianne's mind, but he was also quite sure that once Zeina had an idea in her head, there was no stopping her.

Moving slowly and as carefully as he could through the dense smog, Jackson held a gaslight out in front, Zeina following behind. An eerie clanging above made Jackson jump and lift the lamp towards the sound – something he instantly regretted. The lamp illuminated the belly of the baby whale bound up in the metal net, taking up the entire length of the ship. The whale had stopped struggling and somehow this was even more heartbreaking. Its lumina lines were still flashing but slowly, nowhere near as brightly as they had before.

'Keep going, Jackson,' whispered Zeina, gripping his arm. 'There's nothing we can do until we've talked to Viv.'

They crept on until they reached the stern of the ship and knocked on Vivianne's cabin door.

'Come in,' came Vivianne's triumphant voice, which changed instantly to disappointment when she saw who it was.

She was sitting in an armchair playing cards with a few of her crew. None of them looked up from their game as Zeina strode into the room. Jackson shuffled in behind her. Albi croaked cheerfully from Vivianne's shoulder, munching on a biscuit she had fed him and nuzzling into her auburn curls.

'Shut the door behind you, or the smog will get in. Did your bump to the head help you come to your senses, Zeina?'

'Vivianne—' Zeina began before being interrupted.

'I hope you are here to apologise. Such a fuss, and in the middle of a hunt!'

'We are not here to apologise,' Zeina mumbled quietly.

'Excuse me?' Vivianne asked, focusing more on her hand of cards, which she shuffled before placing one down on the table. 'Beat that, Boris!'

'I said, we are not here to apologise,' Zeina repeated loudly. 'I—*We* have come to ask—No . . . to *demand* that you fly back to the pod immediately and let the whale go.'

Vivianne and her crew stopped their game, turned to stare at the children and then every single one of them broke out into rowdy laughter. The noise made Albi startle and fly back to the safety of his cage, where he flapped and croaked.

'You must be joking.' Vivianne smiled as she got up and closed the cage, settling the angry bird with another treat. Then she walked towards them, wiping tears of amusement from her eyes. She tried to put an arm around Zeina, who shrugged her away. 'Look, Zee, I know you've had a hard time today. You're hurt, you're tired and the hunt came as a bit of a shock. Katu shouldn't have wound you up. But if you think that I am going to let the whale go then you must be quite mad.'

'We are not mad. You don't have to do this to the whale any more. Jackson is head of the Willoughby family now and he says he doesn't want the whale.' She looked up at Vivianne's face, her eyes wide and desperate. 'Hamilton, or whoever is forcing you to do this, can't make you anymore.'

There was more raucous braying from the crew but Vivianne was not laughing now. She looked down at Zeina and stroked her bandaged head, and this time Zeina didn't brush her away.

'You are quite certain this is what you want, Zeina?'

'Yes,' she replied unwaveringly.

'And you, Jackson, this is what you want too? You're sure?'

171

'Yes,' Jackson said with relief.

'Well,' Vivianne sighed, turning away from the children and back to face her crew. 'I'm afraid then, there is really only one thing I can do.'

Jackson couldn't believe Zeina had been right after all. Vivianne was going to order the *Raven* to turn around. But then she spoke.

'Boris, Ledway, take Jackson, please. Joel, Wilson, restrain Zeina.'

The crew leapt into action, each one roughly taking hold of a child's arm in a vice-like grip. Zeina and Jackson shouted as they struggled against their captors, but it was useless.

'Boris, take Jackson down to our prison cell in the hull. Put him in there and lock the door.'

'No!' Zeina's yell echoed as Jackson was dragged away into the night.

CHAPTER 21

Zeina struggled desperately against her captors. She managed to kick Joel on the shin with some force, but he simply laughed. 'Come on now, Miss Starborn, no need for that!'

Under Vivianne's instruction, Joel and Wilson flung Zeina down to the floor and exited, locking the door of Steele's cabin behind them to stand guard outside. Zeina and Vivianne were left quite alone.

'Let me out!' Zeina yelled, running at the door and banging against it with all her might. 'Let Jackson go! You can't put him in a cell. He's a Willoughby! Hamilton will go mad when we get back – everyone will!'

Vivianne sighed and returned to her armchair.

'Jackson was never going back, my dearest.'

'What?' Zeina stopped banging and turned to face Vivianne. She was regarding Zeina with an icy stare.

'Jackson was never going to make it back to the Willoughby

173

Whale,' Steele said. 'In fact, Hamilton would be very disappointed if he were to end up back there somehow.'

Make it back – what could she mean? Where else would he go? Vivianne's lips were set in an ugly smirk. It was as if the Vivianne who had been so kind to her and Jackson had completely vanished and a whole new person had replaced her. Old Vivianne had made Zeina feel important, like she could achieve anything she wanted. This new Vivianne was someone who instructed her crew to fire darts at a baby whale, to reel it in while it struggled against the net, someone who had ordered her and Jackson to be restrained. Zeina felt like the very floor she was standing on had been whipped out from under her. Pain, like a dagger, shot through her heart.

Vivianne went over to the table where the card game had been abandoned and pulled open a drawer. She got out a copy of a newspaper article and handed it to Zeina, who couldn't make any sense of what she saw.

'But ... I don't understand,' she stammered, hands shaking.

'Oh, my love, didn't you ever wonder why Hamilton agreed to let his only nephew come on a trip like this? Why he and that spoilt little brat, Herbert, didn't join us?'

'Because they had to stay to run the Willoughby Whale.'

'Hamilton?' Vivianne laughed a deep, throaty cackle,

quite unlike the high, pretty tinkling Zeina was used to hearing from her. 'He's never done a day of work in his life! No, I'm quite sure the Willoughby Whale would run very well without him. The truth is Hamilton simply can't afford to let Jackson take his place in the family business – it would have quite a disastrous impact on his luxurious lifestyle.'

'I . . . don't understand.'

'No, my darling, you wouldn't. You're quite innocent to the ways of the world. Like I was once upon a time.' She sighed. 'You see, now Lord and Lady Willoughby are out of the way, Jackson inherits *everything*: the fleet, the Whale, Willoughby Towers, an enormous fortune. Hamilton burnt through his own inheritance long ago and he and Herbert would be left with nothing. But if Jackson were to, say . . . die, on a dangerous expedition on the Western Continent . . .' She shrugged. 'Well, then all that lovely money goes to them.'

Zeina looked back down at the paper in her hands. It was a copy of a front page of the *Ravenport Herald*. The headline read **"SMOG RAT ATTACK – HEIR TO THE WILLOUGHBY FORTUNE MURDERED"**. There was a large picture from Jackson's birthday party. Hamilton was smiling, holding a champagne glass and had his arm around Jackson, who was flushed and uncomfortable-looking.

Underneath the story began:

Accounts have been received that Jackson Willoughby (pictured here with his beloved uncle) has been killed after a Smog Rat spy infiltrated a sky whale hunting party on the Western Continent. Reports suggest that he was pushed from the Raven, airship of famous explorer Vivianne Steele, into the deadly Forest of Howlingwood while attempting to capture a new sky whale for the Willoughby family. Although his body could not be found, experts agree that no human could survive a fall from such a height. It has been reported that the culprit responsible for pushing poor Jackson to his death was apprehended immediately by Steele's crew and will be handed over to lawkeepers; the perpetrator will receive a lifetime sentence in the Western Mining Grounds with no chance of a pardon. Hamilton Willoughby released a statement yesterday: 'You cannot imagine, after the tragic news of my brother and sister-in-law last week, how I and the rest of the Willoughby family are feeling. The news of Jackson's murder is truly devastating. We ask that lawkeepers are given new powers to investigate and detain anyone with suspected

Smog Rat connections. Although this is truly the saddest of times, it is of some comfort that Jackson died doing what he loved. He was an enormous fan of airships and adventure, and would not have missed this trip for anything in the world. We are relieved that the Smog Rat was arrested quickly and will be punished severely. Another comfort is that a sky whale was successfully captured by Miss Steele and her crew. It will be fitted with the STAN system as soon as they return and will no longer pose a danger to humans. The new "Jackson Willoughby Whale", named in his honour, will open to guests later next year. I know that this is what my brave nephew would have wanted. R.I.P. Jackson. You will be greatly missed.'

Zeina threw the article down as if the paper it was printed on was poisoned.

'You'll see in the top corner that it is dated two days from now. Hamilton is great friends with the editor of the *Ravenport Herald*, an odious toad of a man who will do anything for a bit of cash. It's all been orchestrated very carefully ahead of time. At the right time, I'm to release Albi with a message. He is trained to seek out Hamilton, who will release the article just as soon as he knows all has gone to plan.'

'You're going to *kill* Jackson?' Zeina shouted.

'No, Zeina!' Vivianne laughed. 'We aren't murderers! We just need to make sure he is safely out of the way. I'm planning to drop him off in the Western Mining Grounds tomorrow. I've got some lawkeeper friends down there who can keep him busy for ten years or so. By the time he makes it out, the money will be long gone and he won't be able to persuade anyone that he is Jackson Willoughby. If he can even remember who he is by then. The mining grounds do have a way of addling your brain.'

Zeina felt sick. Everything she knew about the world had been turned upside down.

'But ... how did Hamilton know that Jackson's parents were going to die?'

Vivianne laughed, cupping Zeina's tear-stained face in her hands and stared deep into her eyes. 'Oh, my little Zee! I admit, I had thought you were a teensy bit more streetwise. Hamilton arranged that too, of course. Jackson wasn't supposed to hear about it – it seemed cruel and unnecessary – and if it wasn't for Katu's meddling with the radio, we could have avoided it.'

'Why would *you* do this?' Zeina choked. 'You're an explorer. What have *you* got against Jackson?'

Vivianne laughed again. 'Nothing, my little lamb – nothing at all. I'm doing it for the money. Hamilton will pay me generously for this trip. Enough to upgrade my ship and mean that, finally, I can be my own boss! No more discovering in the names of Aboves – I can go where I like!'

'You can't do this!' Zeina pushed Steele away from her angrily. 'Hamilton can't do this! I won't let you!'

'Ah well, there we have a little problem, one I hope to resolve without any unpleasantness. You were brought along to be the scapegoat, as you can see from the article, but what actually happens to you is up to me.'

Something clicked in Zeina's head. 'I'm meant to be the spy?'

'That's right. I knew you'd get it, you're such a smart girl. We have our spies in Ravenport too, you know. They were on the lookout for a Below; someone ambitious, someone who was brave enough to agree to come along without any fuss. And then there was that rather amazing letter you sent to my fan club – despite not having the money you still "deserved" the membership as you were my biggest fan. Perfect! Your name was substituted so that you would be invited to Jackson's party and then "win" the prize of accompanying him to the Willoughby Whale. And may I say, you were completely the right choice. You really have been marvellous up to this point. Only problem is, I have grown rather fond of you and that does make the next part rather difficult.'

'You're going to ... give me to the lawkeepers?' Zeina stammered and swayed; she would have collapsed altogether were it not that Steele caught her underneath her arm and held her upright.

'Oh no, my poor little Zee ... not necessarily.' She frowned, gently releasing Zeina from her grip and walking back to her armchair. 'No, what happens next is up to *you*. From the moment I met you, Zeina, you have impressed me. You remind me of myself, actually. You'll remember that on the first night we met, I asked you if you were willing to grab opportunities and make the most of them. Well, now I have the most amazing opportunity for you. One I very much hope you will agree to, for everyone's sake.'

She gestured for Zeina to join her at the table, but Zeina didn't move.

'Stand if you wish but please do consider carefully what I am about to say. With the money that Hamilton gives me, I am about to plan my greatest expedition to date. We can improve the engine capacity of the *Raven* above that of any other airship on the planet. I intend to see what lies beyond the Northern Continent, travel distances and go places that no human has before! We will be away several years, I would imagine, and I would very much like you to join the crew, Zeina.'

Zeina opened her mouth to object but Vivianne interrupted her.

'I know, I know. You are going to say that you could never do that to Jackson, blah, blah, blah. But consider what would have happened if we had all returned to the Willoughby Whale. You two have grown close, I can see that. You think you and Jackson are friends now, eh? Well, you're wrong. The moment he got his inheritance, he would have moved to the Upper Atmosphere and left you to rot in Ravenport your entire life. Aboves are all the same.'

As much as Zeina wanted to believe otherwise, she couldn't help but think this was probably true. She had been cruel to Jackson, used him to get what she wanted, and she wouldn't blame him if he wanted nothing more to do with her once the trip was over. There was no way she was going to stay in Ravenport for ever. This week with Steele had opened her eyes to what her life could be, and there was no shutting them now. But the thought of her dad waiting for her to return, him being left in Ravenport all alone, gave her a tightness around her heart, like an icy hand was squeezing it until it burst.

'Jackson is not the same as us and never will be,' Steele continued. 'If you are willing to throw everything away for an Above, I can't stop you, but if you do agree to join us, you could work your way up in the world just like I did, and get

181

your own airship one day. We could even go and pick up your father in a year or so, once things have settled down a little. An airship always needs a talented engineer!'

This was what Zeina had dreamed of her entire life. If someone had told her a few weeks ago that she could join Vivianne Steele's crew, become an adventurer and travel beyond the known world, she knew that she would have done anything to get it. Now her dream was tainted by what she would have to do to achieve it. She knew she could never do that to Jackson or her dad. She did not have to consider Vivianne's offer, not even for one second.

She shook her head firmly.

'I can't come with you. I'll tell everyone what you and Hamilton have done, unless you let Jackson go.'

Vivianne sighed once more. 'I was worried you might say that. I'm disappointed that you would throw this opportunity away, Zeina.' She stood up and rang a little bell on the table. 'I'm afraid you leave me no choice. Joel and Wilson will escort you back to your cabin, where you will be locked inside until we reach the mining grounds tomorrow.'

'No!' Zeina backed herself against the desk as the door opened, but there was no way to escape. Joel and Wilson grabbed her roughly.

'Joel, Wilson, make sure you double-bolt her door and bring me the aerocycle.' A malicious, satisfied smile cracked

Vivianne's beautiful face in two. 'It really is a marvellous invention, Zeina, but you must be quite mad if you think I ever really believed that you invented it by yourself. Maybe your father will be joining you in the mining grounds someday soon, eh? The lawkeepers will certainly want to speak to him. We can't have that technology falling into the wrong hands.'

CHAPTER 22

A murky-green liquid dripped from the low ceiling in front of Jackson, forming a puddle on the floor. The dank cell was dark save for a few narrow stripes of light from the gaps in the barred window. A deep graze on his arm burned with pain – an injury from Boris and Ledway shoving him down the narrow stairwell to the hull.

Jackson huddled, his head between his knees, fists balled in frustration. He was angry – with Boris and Ledway, with Vivianne, with Hamilton, but more than anything he was angry with himself; he had known all along that there was something wrong about this trip but he had let himself be bullied by Zeina and charmed by Vivianne, and let his guard down. Now, they were trapped. Where was Zeina now? Was she safe?

Jackson pulled at the threadbare blanket round his shoulders and shivered. It hadn't eluded him that it would be very convenient for Hamilton if he were to disappear, especially now his parents were gone. He cursed himself again – they should have gone to Katu instead. He felt sure now that the Kotarth was their only chance of escape.

A loud metallic CLUNK on the side of the hull stirred him from his thoughts. The whole airship wobbled, an eerie clanking echoing somewhere above him. There were other noises too – shouting, banging, screeching. He stood up, straining to hear, but the sounds were muffled by the thick cell walls. The airship rocked again. Voices, angry but indistinguishable, drifted down the stairwell and then footsteps, heavier than before, and a familiar jangling of iron keys. Jackson hurried to his feet. He wasn't sure what he was going to do but he knew he had to do something. His whole life he had done what he was told. He'd been bossed around by his parents, his tutor, Mrs Hogwood, Hamilton and even Zeina – he never stood up for himself. Enough was enough!

He knelt down in the darkest corner of the cell, a plan forming in his head. If he could just get Boris to step inside, maybe he could run at the door. Then he could bolt the door behind him, trapping Boris inside and maybe, just maybe, get to Katu. It was a long shot but his only one.

Eventually, there was a fumble of keys and the heavy bolt clanked open.

'Oh!' Jackson couldn't help gasping in surprise.

185

A giant bear-like man was silhouetted in the door frame. He bowed his enormous shoulders to step inside, the ceiling skimming the top of his tricorn hat. Underneath, shaggy black hair tumbled into a tangled salt-and-pepper beard. In one hand gleamed a curved silver cutlass and at his waist he held a black pistol.

'Jackson Willoughby,' boomed a gruff voice. 'Come with me.'

CHAPTER 23

Zeina's whole body ached. Whether it was from her fall during the hunt, the way Joel and Wilson had wrestled her back to her cabin, or the hours she had spent since, launching herself stubbornly at the bolted door, she wasn't sure. A wild temper raged within her with every punch and kick, but the real source of her anger remained unclear. She was certainly furious with Vivianne – her smug face swam into view, making Zeina roar – but she was, possibly, even angrier with herself.

Her father had warned her, Shrapnel had warned her, yet, as usual, she had launched herself headlong into trouble. Worse than that, she had taken Jackson along with her and now both their lives were in danger. How could she have been so naive to have believed Steele actually cared about her? Why had she not asked more questions about hunting sky whales and blindly believed everything she'd read? Desperate tears fell down her face as she thought of her own dad, waiting for her to never return. Maybe that was how the parents of the captured baby whale felt too.

In her fury, she had banged her head and now fresh blood was seeping through the bandage and dripping down her nose. She hadn't had water, food or sleep for what seemed like days. Exhausted, she collapsed into a restless slumber on her cabin floor.

*

She woke to the sound of chaos. Feet thundered on the deck above, followed by shouts, bangs, clanks, thuds and someone, somewhere, yelping in pain. The whale was rattling its net, making a low desperate moan, as the giant crane whined and creaked. The smell of burning wood rose above the fatty stench of her cabin.

There was a clamour of heavy footsteps and then a blaze of light from the gap under her door. Someone was just outside her cabin. Someone with large boots and a gas lamp.

'Miss Starborn. Step away from the door, please. Get right back, as far as you can go.'

She recognised the cool, calm voice of Katu and felt instantly furious.

'Why should I do anything *you* tell me to do?'

'Because I am here to save your life.'

Seeing as she had very few other options, Zeina did as she was told. There was a loud bang, a dazzling flash and then a clank as the bolt fell to the floor. The door swung open and there was Katu in his travelling cloak. His companion held a smoking pistol in one hand and a gas lamp in the other. She wore a long leather coat with gold buttons and brocade right up to the collar and a matching cocked hat. Most of her face was concealed one way or another – her nose and mouth by a large respirator mask, and her eyes, well, one of them at least, hidden behind a sort of goggle-monocle contraption. The other eye was not in need of protection as it was missing altogether. The ragged edges of the scar where her left eye should have been made Zeina recoil. Perhaps most fascinating was the fact that the arm holding the gas lamp was not an arm at all – well, not a human one anyway. In its place was a metal prosthesis, made from scrap and cogs and pipes that were all fitted together to form the metal skeleton of an arm and hand. The places where the metal bones touched were thick with black grease.

'Come on, girly! There'll be time enough for staring at my ugly mug when we're safe. Where's the boy?'

'Jackson?' Zeina asked, mesmerised by the enormous woman. She was undeniably the woman from that Wanted poster – a Smog Rat! Despite this, there was something rather comforting in her blunt tone and fearsome appearance.

'Well, I don't mean the blooming King of the Ice Bears, do I, girly?' The woman shrugged, rolling her eye at Katu.

'They locked him in a cell down in the hull.'

'Jamie! He's in the hull,' the woman whispered to a man behind her. 'You've got five minutes, no more, or I'll leave you both behind.'

She replaced her pistol in a holster she wore around her waist and got a spare pair of goggles and a respirator from the inside of her coat. Zeina was a little disappointed that these were handed to her using the human arm.

'Not a sound. You understand? Keep your questions for the *Nightjar*.'

'The *Nightjar*?'

'Our airship. From now on you keep your head down, your mouth shut and do exactly what you're told, yes?'

Deciding that, for once, it was probably best just to follow instructions, Zeina nodded. Katu pulled up his hood and Zeina grabbed her backpack. The one-eyed woman lowered her hat, turned down the gas lamp to a gentle orange glow, and the three of them crept silently up the stairs to the main deck.

Peeking above the floorboards, the sounds that had woken Zeina from her cabin floor became clear. The deck was in absolute chaos. The *Raven* had been bordered by another airship that had anchored itself to the starboard side. This airship wasn't as sleek as Vivianne's, but was impressive all the same. A rounded cockpit of glass and steel made up the bow and to its stern was bolted a large bulbous chamber. Sheets of scrap metal had been welded together to form a forked rudder underneath and two magnificent articulated wings at either side. Ladders had been laid down between the two crafts, and men and women from the invading airship were clambering on to the deck of the *Raven*, some brandishing swords and others firing pistols into the air.

The *Raven*'s night shift had obviously been taken completely by surprise. Some crewmembers were running in all directions shouting and trying to raise the alarm, while others appeared to have only just woken up. Heads poked out of cabins, dazed or wrestling with respirators in the darkness and confusion. Towards the bow of the ship, someone had dropped and smashed a gas lamp and, exposed to the toxic smog, flames were now spreading over floorboards and licking up the railings. In the centre of the deck was Boris, huddled on the floor, holding his leg and yowling like an injured cat. A man wearing a pointed hat like the one-eyed woman stood there turning the winch that controlled the crane and the baby whale was hanging in mid-air above the two ships. Lumina lines flashing, it struggled against the net, making the crane whine and both airships rock back and forth violently. Wilson, the woman who had so roughly imprisoned Zeina in her cabin, had managed to find her goggles, respirator and pistol. She was firing towards the man in the pointed hat, who ducked and fired back but did not stop turning the crane. Just when Zeina thought nothing else could possibly happen, Vivianne appeared, silhouetted against the flames. She was wearing her white furs and holding one of the dart guns. She fired and an enormous dart sailed past their heads, narrowly missing the man at the crane.

'Get over to that winch, Wilson. Boris, stop howling and help! Ledway, Jem, get the other dart guns.'

'Heavens!' the Smog Rat woman hissed, grabbing her pistol from its holster. 'I'd better go and help. You two, get aboard while you can. Keep to the shadows and move quick.'

'Wait.' Zeina had suddenly remembered something. 'I need to get my aerocycle!'

'What nonsense is this? Anything that isn't on your person right now isn't coming with you.'

'But Steele has it! She said something about it falling into the wrong hands. About capturing my dad . . .'

'Where is the aerocycle, Zeina?' asked Katu.

'Steele's cabin, I think.'

Katu turned to face the woman. 'We should retrieve the aerocycle, Parr. Steele mustn't find out how it works.'

'Fine,' Parr said. 'Meet you on the *Nightjar*. But I'll be leaving as soon as that whale is secured, whether you're aboard or not.' She loaded her pistol and ventured out into the mayhem of the deck.

It took Zeina and Katu less than a minute to reach the stern of the ship. Katu was an expert at finding shadows to slip into and they managed to get there unnoticed by the panicking crew. Steele's cabin was unlocked and completely deserted apart from Albi's cage. The bird hissed at Katu as he rifled through chests and ransacked shelves. Zeina went through every drawer in the card table but her aerocycle was nowhere to be found.

'Katu, this one is locked.' It was the drawer from which Steele had got the newspaper article. Zeina pulled and pushed and rattled, but to no avail.

'Sssh! You're making far too much noise!' Katu opened his cloak and from a little pocket on the inside drew out a key. It was long and thin and fit perfectly into the lock with a little click.

'You have a key to Steele's drawer?' Zeina whispered.

'It's a skeleton key – it can open any lock on the four continents.'

They opened the drawer and there was her beloved aerocycle alongside the *Ravenport Herald* article. She placed them both in her pack.

'We should take Albi, too. Vivianne said something about him delivering messages to Hamilton.'

Katu nodded. 'Best if you hold the cage, I think. Albi doesn't seem to know that Kotarth are vegetarian.'

The bird jumped and flapped as Zeina held the cage, rocking it back and forth and making an enormous racket. They were about to retreat back to the shadows of the deck when they heard the click of a pistol being cocked.

'Don't move,' said Joel. 'Put down the bird and I'm taking you both to Viv. Do it now – or I'll shoot!'

'Mr Joel, we have no weapons and I ask respectfully that you let us go.'

'Now, why would I do that?' His voice was uncertain, shaken.

'Because if you don't let us leave with that ship, Steele will kill me and send Zeina here to the mining grounds, where she too will probably die.'

Joel's hand, the one that was holding the pistol, began to quiver uncontrollably when Katu mentioned the mining grounds.

'I can't do that, Katu. Even if I wanted to.'

'Joel!' Zeina shouted, making Joel direct his pistol at her face. 'She's going to send me and Jackson to die in the mining grounds. You've been there! I know you wouldn't want that!'

The old airman began to sniff but did not lower the shaking pistol.

'We had none of this in the olden days. None of this spying or murdering! What's wrong with a good old-fashioned whale hunt, eh? Killing whales is all well and good, but this? I'm not cut out for killing humans. Or cat-bear people . . . whatever you are, Katu.'

Katu's furry brow furrowed but evidently decided that now was not the time to explain the origins of the Kotarth. He took one large step between Zeina and Joel, his paws reaching out slowly to hold Joel's shaking hands. The shipman stiffened and for a moment Zeina thought he might fire straight through Katu's chest. She froze, too terrified to move.

'Oh . . . off with you,' Joel breathed suddenly, throwing his pistol down in disgust. 'Go on – before I change my mind. And don't be telling Viv if you get caught, or it'll be me back in the mining grounds and I wouldn't make it out this time.'

He collapsed, defeated, into a chair, leaving Katu to scoop Zeina back into the shadows. By now, most of the *Raven* crew were out on deck too, either facing off the intruders or trying to put out the flames. There were blasts from pistols and the occasional bolt from a dart gun being fired. The crane's arm now stretched over to the waiting *Nightjar*, and the baby whale, still in its net, was being unhooked and secured to the deck.

'Quick, Miss Starborn, we've got seconds until those ladders are taken up!'

Zeina's heart lifted when she spotted Jackson, already aboard, looking out anxiously into the mayhem. The crew of the *Nightjar* were retreating, firing their pistols as they did, and Katu grabbed Zeina's arm, breaking into a run. There was no hiding in the shadows now, not with a clanking, flapping, croaking Albi in tow.

'Wilson, Ledway, fire!' Vivianne pointed to the pair. 'Don't let them get away!'

Darts flew past Katu's head, but he did not stop running. Zeina's head throbbed and her arm ached under the weight of the golden cage, but she didn't stop either. They reached the *Nightjar* just as the last of the ladders were being taken up and threw themselves across. As the airship began to rise, Zeina toppled into a terrified Jackson, wrapping both her arms round his neck.

'No time for reunions now, you two. Get down and stay down. They won't let us go that easy,' Parr shouted. 'Extra power! Get down there, Beard! Ascend! Swift turn north. Atkins, give them a hand with that winch.' Her crew responded in an instant.

The *Nightjar* rose almost vertically and then turned in the air with an agility Zeina had not seen in any airship before. They were heading away from the smog layer and into the Upper Atmosphere.

'Impressive, isn't it?' The captain winked at Zeina and

Jackson. 'It's fast too. Much faster than the *Raven*. Still, we won't be a match for their—'

The *Nightjar* jolted suddenly, sending the crew off their feet. There was an almighty bang of metal on metal and black smoke billowed from somewhere near the stern of the ship.

'HARPOON! Quick! Turn east. It'll take them longer to change course. Now! Before they have a chance to reload!'

CHAPTER 24

Jackson closed his eyes as the *Nightjar* darted from east to west, north to south. He could hear the frantic whirring of winches, the creaking of the enormous metal wings with every roll and yaw. Every so often, there was a wail from the *Raven* behind them, the whoosh of the great harpoon, shouts of 'DUCK!' or 'INCOMING!' and then thuds all around him, as everyone hit the deck for cover.

But the *Nightjar* was indeed faster than the *Raven* and much more agile, weaving through the toxic smog, changing direction again and again until, eventually, the roar of their pursuers became lost in the clouds.

'It's all right, Jackson, open your eyes!' said Zeina, shaking him gently as his nausea began to ease. 'We're safe! Come on! There are a few things you need to see.'

Jackson wasn't sure Zeina's definition of "safe" was quite the same as his. In the last twenty-four hours, they had been chased by an angry sky whale, imprisoned by the people who were supposed to be looking after them, kidnapped by Smog Rats (probably the very same ones who had killed his parents), narrowly avoided bullets, darts and a deck fire, and then just about survived a harpoon strike!

He opened his eyes nevertheless and hesitantly got to his feet, choosing to follow Zeina towards the stern rather than remain alone surrounded by their fearsome captors.

From here he could see the outline of the whole airship, silhouetted against brightening clouds. Each of the steel wings were now fully extended as the airship soared upwards. Somehow, they managed to look both powerful and elegant, enormous Vs stretching into tapered tips.

'Amazing, isn't it?' Zeina's eyes were bright and excited behind her goggles. 'Look, down here too.'

Below the railings of the main deck stretched a network of metal bars and poles and suspended at intervals from these were what looked like at least twenty velocycles. They each possessed their own panting rider, cycling in mid-air. Where the wheels should have been were belts and generators, and below them a sea of enormous propellers, whirring at full speed and churning up the smog like butter. How they could keep cycling at such speed with that terrifying drop below them was beyond Jackson. At the very back hung a huge rudder that balanced the ship. It moved gracefully from side to side with every pitch of the bow, rather like the tail of a giant fish.

'There's something else I need to show you,' Zeina said gently. Biting her lip, she took a folded piece of newspaper from her pocket with trembling hands and handed it to him. It took him a while to realise what he was reading.

'W-Where did you get this?' he stuttered. It didn't make any sense.

'Steele showed it to me. Hamilton had it written before we even left.'

He listened as Zeina explained, his mind reeling, then collapsed weakly against the deck, stomach swirling, fists clenched and quivering.

'How could he do this? To his *own brother*.' But deep down Jackson knew there would have been little point in getting rid of him without first eliminating his parents. Now, Hamilton and Herbert would get everything.

Zeina crouched down next to him, putting her arm around his shoulders. 'I'm so sorry, Jackson.'

The Smog Rats may not have killed his parents, but the sight of their captain striding towards them still made his heart race. She had taken off her hat to reveal a crop of messy brown hair, a patch of which was missing altogether. The scorched skin underneath stretched down to where her left eye should have been. Leaning over the railings, she bellowed down to the riders.

'Ease off now, Beard!'

A lad, no more than a year older than Jackson, turned his face up to her. 'Right you are, Penny!'

'That's Captain Parr to you,' she growled.

He laughed. 'All right, boss! We need a break. The harpoon's blown a hole in the smog chamber but we've managed to patch it up.'

'We're about to break the cloud layer,' she called back. 'Enjoy a break from your respirators too, while you can.'

The wings dipped and the *Nightjar* burst through the last clouds into the limitless blue above. The glow of a new dawn reflected off the airship's wings and now Jackson could see that they were painted in swirling patterns of silver and grey – camouflage for the smog, he supposed. Captain Parr found a barrel near the children, sat down and took off her mono-goggle and respirator. She gestured for them to do the same and then handed them each some biscuits and a canteen of fresh water from inside her coat.

'Won't Steele have a better chance of finding us up here?' Zeina asked, after devouring four biscuits at once. Jackson wasn't sure he was brave enough to even speak to the captain, let alone question her judgement. With an ominous clunk, she unbolted her mechanical arm and rubbed at the red skin underneath.

'We'll be able to see her coming too, remember,' she explained. 'Plus the whale needs a break from the smog.'

The baby whale was still confined to its metal net but had a little more space to move its flippers. It was being given an injection by the big bear of a man who had freed Jackson from his cell.

'Probably didn't introduce himself when he blasted open your cell, but that's Jamie. Might look like a beast but he's dead soft, I promise.' She smiled.

Jackson watched him stroking the baby whale's giant nose.

'He was a scientist, once upon a time,' Parr continued. 'Used to work at the STANS facility, setting up the system on the whales when they were small. There came a day when he just couldn't stomach it anymore – so he found us.'

Jackson guiltily gulped down some water; his grandfather had set up that facility. He began to worry that gentle Jamie might make an exception for him, once he knew he was a Willoughby. The blood drained from his face.

Parr looked at Jackson and laughed heartily. 'It's all right, lad! Katu has told us who you are.' She looked straight into his pale face with her eye, which, now her monocle had been removed, Jackson could see was piercingly dark – the colour of a midnight sky. 'Haven't you ever wondered how your STAN system works, Master Willoughby?'

Jackson shook his head.

'Turns them into robots,' she explained. 'Takes over all their motor functions. They know full well what's going on.

They're desperate to escape, but can't – trapped like that until they die.'

Zeina spat out the biscuit she was munching on. Jackson felt sick. The mechanism of the STAN system was a closely guarded secret, but his textbooks had always made it sound like it helped the whales, keeping them calm and happy. The truth repulsed him.

'I'm not a Willoughby anymore,' he said, fidgeting. 'I'm dead.' He threw the *Ravenport Herald* he was still holding under the captain's nose. She studied it carefully.

'Well, with family like that who needs enemies, eh?' Parr grabbed Jackson's shoulder. 'Anyone who Steele wants dead is all right by me, lad. Katu said so anyway, and I trust that Kotarth completely.'

Zeina snorted rudely. Parr took a small tub of black grease from the inside of her jacket and placed her mechanical arm in her lap. Taking a little of the grease, she began to work it into each joint and cog, bending each of the fingers gently. She regarded Zeina sceptically.

'Still don't trust him then? Even after he saves you and your friend and rescues your aerogywhatsit? Hard to please, aren't you, girly?'

'It's him who doesn't like me,' Zeina grumbled. 'It's because I'm a Below.'

'And who do you think I am? Empress of the Southern

Continent? We're all Belows on here! Well, present company excluded.' She mock-saluted Jackson. 'No, he likes you all right. It's just you remind him of Steele and there's someone he does hate, with a passion.'

'Why track the whales for her then?' Zeina asked.

'That's his story to tell. But he cares about sky whales more than any of us here. He's got this connection with them; all Kotarth do. Breaks his heart every time. He feels their pain as if it's his own.'

A movement just out of Jackson's eyeline – a scurry of white; a silent gasp – caused him to turn suddenly. Someone was spying on them from behind some crates, a small person who had ducked the moment his head turned. He could spot two little hands, a forehead, long spikes of white-blonde hair that stuck up as if they had been electrocuted and the occasional peep of two dark-brown eyes.

'It's all right, Sparks, come on out,' said Parr, beckoning gently. 'These two won't hurt you.'

There was a sharp intake of breath, before Sparks darted out from behind the crates and raced away in the opposite direction.

'Don't worry, she'll warm to you. A nervous little thing, but that's to be expected, I suppose. She's friendly in her own way, once she knows you a bit.'

'Who is she?' Jackson judged the speedy little figure must be no more than ten years old.

'Don't know for sure. Found her locked in the STANS room when we raided one of the whales. She's been with us ever since. A useful little thing too – excellent at fixing anything electrical, no matter how broken.'

'Won't she tell you what happened to her?' asked Jackson.

'I've never heard a word out of her mouth – not one.'

'She doesn't talk at all?' asked Zeina.

'She'll whisper the odd word now and then to Jamie, but that's it. It's not our place to pry – she'll tell us when she's ready, if she can.'

They all fell silent for a while, watching Jamie tending to the whale and the crew of the *Nightjar* clearing the airship of debris and making repairs as best they could.

'So, what now?' Zeina asked.

'Get this baby back to its pod before they disappear. Katu says they're still waiting over the forest. But they won't stay much longer – too risky for them. After that it's back to raiding as many whale hotels as we can. You've read the newspaper articles. We Smog Rats ambush whales, destroy, steal, beat up "noble" lawkeepers and terrify passengers and crew alike.' She winked at them, which looked strange considering her one-eyed-ness.

'And do you . . . kill people?' Jackson asked, staring as Parr bolted her arm back in place and began to flex each silver finger slowly.

'Course not! There are two sides in this world, lad – those who want things to stay as they are and those who are fighting for change. We are the latter and we are growing all the time. We have spies embedded all across the continents and our very own Innovator, designing superior technology. But the other side have a lot to lose and the lawmakers, lawkeepers and newspapers are on their side. You can't believe everything you read in the papers.' She gave him a nudge, holding up the copy of the *Ravenport Herald*. 'We don't attack people. And we only steal what we need to survive.'

'Is that how you get the ore you need? You steal it?' Jackson asked. It was something he'd been curious about ever since he first heard reports of the Smog Rat attacks.

'Who says we need ore?' Parr said. 'You've seen our smog chamber – it uses the smog from the atmosphere as fuel and then we've got cycle power when we need a boost. This whole ship is a revelation. Our Innovator could transform the world. But right now it's safer if no one, not even me, knows their true identity. If they were found out, the lawmakers would make sure they were never seen again.'

Jackson noticed that Zeina was uncharacteristically quiet, staring blankly into the sky, frowning with her freckled nose crinkled in that way she always did when she was thinking hard about something.

'Our ultimate mission is to free every sky whale,' continued Parr. 'Let them make their way back to their pods if they can, and die in peace if they can't. Jamie says wild sky whales can live for up to three hundred years above the limits of the Upper Atmosphere. The ones fitted with STAN systems last eighty at most.'

A racket from the bow made them all turn suddenly.

'Parr!' bellowed Jamie. 'You'll want to hear this!'

Parr's metallic joints creaked as she sprang up from her seat, running the length of the deck with Zeina and Jackson close behind her.

On reaching the cockpit, Jackson could see that everyone was crowded around a battered radiograph. They parted as the captain entered and pushed her way to the front where Sparks sat on a little stool, expertly moving the dials back and forth. There was a buzz, a crackle, and then a voice came through, but only for a second. Zeina gasped beside him. The gauges were alight, needles moving back and forth, as Sparks tried to tune in.

'Get it back, Sparks!' yelled Parr.

Sparks fiddled with the wires and then gave the radiograph a sharp little tap with her fist. The voice was back: '9229 . . . MAYDAY . . . STRANDED . . . BUZZZZZZZ.'

And then it disappeared again. The lights went off suddenly; the dials fell still. And this time no amount of tuning or fiddling or tapping could get it back.

'Who was that?' Jackson asked the silent room.

The crew were watching Parr intently. 'The Innovator has an emergency code that changes constantly – 9229 is the latest. Thirty-six hours ago, we got a mayday call. 9229 and their scout were trapped in thunder-fog over the Western Mountains. The Innovator is under strict instructions to stay undercover at all times. I can't understand why they would risk themselves like that, but we need to rescue them.'

'Zeina? What's wrong?' Jackson asked, grabbing her shoulders. He noticed how pale she was, paler even than when she had banged her head and passed out on Steele's ship. She was shaking, staring right through him as if he wasn't there at all.

'I know,' she said quietly.

'What?' Jackson had never seen her look so terrified – not in the face of pistols or dart guns or harpoons or even a sky whale – and it unnerved him.

'I know,' she said, louder this time so that everyone could hear. 'I know who the Innovator is.'

CHAPTER 25

Zeina felt as if pieces of a puzzle had been shuffling into place for a while, and now, after hearing that voice, they were locking together. A cold dread crept through her.

Jackson gasped, looking terrified. 'What do you mean, Zeina? How do you know?'

She couldn't speak, couldn't make her mouth form the words. The whole crew were staring at her. Captain Parr broke the silence. 'Come on then, girly, you'd better start talking.' Her voice was sharp, fixing Zeina with a dark, one-eyed glare.

Zeina took a deep breath.

'I think my aerocycle might work the same way as your smog chamber,' she began hesitantly.

'Impossible,' Parr interjected, watching Zeina closely. 'This is the only ship of its kind, the first to fly without ore. The only way your aeromagigamy could work the same way is if the Innovator themselves had made it – something they would *never* do. It would put our entire mission in grave danger.'

Zeina gulped and opened her pack. Taking out her aerocycle, she folded out the parts to show how it worked. The crew crowded in closer.

'This is the part that makes it fly,' Zeina said, pointing to the stolen part.

'It flies?' Parr demanded, raising her eyebrow to look at Katu.

He nodded solemnly.

The captain sucked in her teeth, grabbing the aerocycle from Zeina's hands. 'Well, I can see now, Katu, why you risked so much to retrieve it. I'm no engineer but this part looks like a miniature version of our smog chamber.'

She handed the aerocycle to Katu and folded her arms, human over mechanical. Zeina felt Jackson trembling next to her, she couldn't look him in the eye.

'Thank heavens Steele wasn't able to find out how it worked. If she had, well . . .' Parr's voice trailed off and she shook her head, before fixing Zeina with another fierce glare. 'What you need to tell us now is where you got that part from.'

'I . . . I stole it,' Zeina mumbled.

The crew gasped. Parr's eye burned blue. Jackson gripped Zeina's hand in his.

'I'm sorry . . .' she stuttered. 'I didn't know that it was a secret. I just found it with some airship plans and knew that it would work perfectly. So I took it.'

'That means you also know another piece of top-secret information, girly – one that I don't even know. Whoever left the plans and this part around for you to steal . . . must be our Innovator.'

Zeina burst into tears. 'I . . . It's not his fault though! He didn't know. He wouldn't have known until he found me gone – until Shrapnel told him how I got away.' Tears streamed down her face. 'It's my dad. I stole the part from his drawer. And that was his voice on the radio – I would know it anywhere.' She didn't understand: her steady, sensible father, who never did anything other than what he was told, who wouldn't even let her go on an airship. How could he have been working with the Smog Rats all along?

'You won't hurt him, will you? It wasn't his fault, it was mine. He—'

Parr hushed her. She placed her hands on Zeina's shoulders – one warm and human, the other cool and mechanical, but both kindly, somehow.

'He is in danger, Zeina, but not from us.'

'What?' Panic cracked Zeina's chest in two. 'But we can save him! Sparks can get the radio working. We can go and get him . . .'

Parr took a deep breath and shook her head. 'The message

we got from the scout two days ago explained that they were lost in a thunder-fog storm in an unidentified ship. We couldn't understand why they had blown their covers, why they had set off in the first place, but now . . . Well, a few things make a little bit more sense.'

Zeina remembered how frantic Shrapnel said her dad had been after she left. She remembered writing that stupid letter to him on the Willoughby Whale. Had Shrapnel told him about the aerocycle then? Or had her dad already discovered the missing part? Deep down she knew what Parr and everyone else knew – her dad had put himself, and the Smog Rats, in terrible danger for her. He'd risked everything to try and rescue her.

'They were over the Western Mountains,' Parr continued. 'Somewhere near the border to the mining grounds, close to where we were hiding, waiting to hear news from Katu.'

Two days ago – that wouldn't have been long before the *Raven* passed through the mining grounds. Zeina remembered how that lawkeeper had beamed with pride as he told Steele about the thunder-fog. She felt sick. She had been so close to her dad then. He'd been in danger because of her, and yet she hadn't even been thinking about him, so concerned was she with impressing Vivianne.

'So what have you done to find them?' She tried to keep her voice even and strong, but it kept wavering.

'Nothing, Zeina. They didn't give their coordinates in time. We could never search an area that big while staying undercover. The message from Katu about you and Jackson and the baby whale came in shortly after. We prioritise the lives of innocents above that of our scouts. All of us sign up knowing that our lives will be put in danger – a risk we happily take on for the cause.'

'But we have to go and find them now.' It felt like someone had taken all the breath from Zeina's lungs. Jackson was frozen to the spot, staring at her, his pale face horror-stricken.

'We can't do that, Zeina. I'm sorry.'

'But we have to!' she shouted, pushing out against the sea of people surrounding her. Their faces swam, drowned by her tears.

'I'm sorry, Zeina. I know this is hard, but there really is nothing we can do. Without their exact location we wouldn't know where to start. It could take days, weeks even, and Steele would find us first. Even if Sparks got the radio back, even if they managed to tell us their coordinates – the whale just wouldn't make it. The Innovator cares very much about our cause . . .'

Zeina was now sobbing uncontrollably. Her words came in gasps of despair. 'But he's not the Innovator . . . he's my dad.'

Zeina couldn't take it any more – the shock in the faces of the crew, the pity radiating from Parr, Jackson's useless wide-eyed horror, Katu standing there as still and emotionless as ever.

'You don't know anything about him!' she screamed at them all. She turned from the cockpit and ran.

CHAPTER 26

'**R**ight then, lad. This moping about isn't going to help anyone, is it?'

Jamie's gruff voice broke through Jackson's thoughts. Hearing about Zeina's father had come as a big shock. He had run after her, tried to comfort her, but Zeina was determined to be alone.

'What do you want me to do?' Jackson asked, his eyes red and sore.

'I'll need some extra help if I'm going to keep this whale alive long enough to get it back to its mum. Come on, you can help us feed it. Should think the poor thing is starving.'

Sparks hovered behind Jamie's large frame, glaring at Jackson suspiciously as he led the way to the net. She tugged at Jamie's sleeve and he bent down so she could whisper into his ear. He laughed, ruffling her spiked head. 'I'll make sure, don't worry!' Her expression did not change as Jamie passed Jackson a giant glass bottle filled with murky brown liquid.

'Right, take off the lid and put this on.' He handed him a long rubber tube with a bung at one end. 'Then you just pop the tube in its mouth and tip the bottle up! Easy!'

Jackson was more than a little hesitant to be anywhere near the whale's enormous mouth. The smell of rotting fish hit him full in the face when he removed the bottle top, causing him to hold his breath and pull up his shirt to try and cover his nose and mouth. Sparks sniggered.

'Ahhhh! What is this stuff?' he asked.

'It's what they pump into the whales' stomachs to keep them alive. I stole a load of the stuff during our last raid. Haven't you ever wondered what the whales eat?'

'But what is it? It smells awful!'

'Preserved fish guts, mainly. Wild whales eat sky fish. The Upper Atmosphere used to have whole shoals of them but, just like the sky whales, they've disappeared. We think sky whales do most of their feeding in the far regions of the distant continents now – anywhere that isn't polluted enough to have killed all the sky fish. This little one here should be on its mother's milk really.'

Jackson stuck the rubber bung into the bottle top as quickly as he could, in the hope that it might ease the smell. 'Eurgh!'

'Yep! But it's all this little one's got at the moment, so get on with it!'

Jackson thought the term "little one" was an odd choice, the baby whale being as long as the airship itself. He carefully walked around one of the paddle-like flippers to reach its head and then knelt down so he was level with its great mouth. Each of the pointed teeth emerging from the rubbery lips was easily the size of Jackson's arm.

'Just pull up the lip and pop in the end of the tube. He'll open up his mouth a bit more once he works out it's food. Must be starving, poor thing.'

Jackson hesitated; the whale opening his mouth was what he was worried about! But, not wanting to disappoint Jamie or prove Sparks right, he shut his eyes, lifted up the great grey lip and pushed the tube between two of the huge teeth.

'There you go! I think he likes you – just look at his lumina lines.'

The whale's markings were beginning to light up with a gentle glow that spread up and down each flipper. The mouth opened a little and Jackson fed in a little more of the rubber tube.

'He definitely likes you, lad. This can be your job. The whale will need feeding every few hours. It'll need all the energy it can get for when we make it back to the pod. What do you think, Sparks? Do we trust him with our precious cargo?'

The tiny girl did not reply, but she did step out from

behind Jamie's leg to get a closer look. She was a scraggy little thing – short but also gangly somehow, with long skinny arms and legs sticking out from overalls at least three sizes too big for her. The sleeves and legs had been rolled up many times so that they didn't drag on the floor. Her face was thin, making her dark eyes look enormous. With a tiny smile and a curt nod to Jamie she was gone, disappearing to some other hiding place.

'Looks like you've passed!'

'Um ... thanks.' Jackson wasn't thrilled about his new post, but after what his family had done to the sky whales over the years, he felt it was the least he could do.

'And now for that bird. What do you call him? Albi? Poor thing needs to be let out of that golden prison immediately!'

Jackson panicked. 'Oh! Be careful. He's rather ... er ... grumpy.'

Jamie scoffed. 'Wouldn't you be, shut up in a tiny space like that? Ice Ravens fly for hundreds of miles in the wild – it's inhumane to keep him locked up! I'm letting him out right away. Parr? You agree?'

'Go on, Jamie. Open it up,' the captain yelled from the cockpit. 'We'll just have to take our chances that he might fly back to Steele or Hamilton. Nobody on my ship will be kept in a prison.'

Jamie approached the cage and unlocked the door. Albi

croaked suspiciously, but with a little gentle coaxing, stepped one white feathery foot and then the other on to Jamie's overalled arm. He flapped a little and then spread out his magnificent crystal wings. With a ruffle of feathers and a stretching of claws, he took off and Jackson saw, for the second time, the amazing transformation of an Ice Raven in flight. He soared, a diamond flash against the clear blue sky, into the endless freedom above.

CHAPTER 27

Zeina sat alone for many hours, her eyes red and raw. She wouldn't let anyone near her, not even Jackson. She sat, legs dangling over the ship's bow, her face aching as she stared blankly into the afternoon sky.

It was getting dark by the time Katu approached Zeina. He brought her a gas lamp and spare coat to drape around her shoulders and keep out the cool evening air – neither of which she accepted or thanked him for.

'I have come to express my deepest sympathies, Miss Starborn.'

Zeina did not reply. She continued to stare into the evening dusk.

'I also want you to know that I thought a great deal of the Innovator. I never had the opportunity to meet him in person, but I had a great appreciation for his work. The *Nightjar* is a revelation.'

'Don't call him that. And don't talk about him as if he's

dead!' Zeina snapped.

'I apologise, Miss Starborn. But I'm afraid to say, whatever happens, your family is neither the first nor the last to have suffered greatly for our cause.'

'What would you know?'

Katu's black nostrils flared, his beard bristled, but his voice remained gentle. He came and sat down next to her. She shuffled away, turning her back to him.

'I wanted to explain to you why I worked for Steele. You need to understand what is at stake for every one of us who agrees to join the Smog Rats. Your father, I'm certain, would have considered this carefully before joining.'

'Don't talk about him like you knew him. You didn't.' *Neither did I*, Zeina thought miserably, her head hunched over her knees. If she hadn't heard his voice herself on that radio, she would never have believed that her father would join something so dangerous. Everything he did, he did to keep her safe, whether she wanted him to or not. Joining the Smog Rats seemed so alien to what she knew to be one of his core beliefs.

'I don't presume to know him, Miss Starborn, but I think my story may help you to see what all of us, including your father, are fighting for.'

She shrugged, too tired to fight anymore.

'I am ashamed to say that Miss Steele has a great power over me,' he continued solemnly. 'She herself has probably told you that I am a Prince of the Kotarth – she enjoys boasting about it – but what she will not have said is that she holds my whole race as hostages against me.'

Despite herself, Zeina's interest was piqued. She turned her head to peer at the Kotarth. His ears were flattened and his golden eyes shone with tears, pupils widened into black pools.

'When she arrived in our forest – "Howlingwood", as she calls it – it was five times the size it is now. She cut down our trees to blast holes in the earth in search of ore. Trees were replaced by furnaces, funnels and machines. More and more of our forest was mined until there was only a small part of what we call home remaining.'

Katu's sadness cut through Zeina's own, reaching her in a way that kind words never could. She turned to face him. 'Why didn't you fight back? Try to stop her?'

'The Kotarth are a peace-loving species and, until then, the forest had protected us. We didn't have weapons; we didn't know what to do.' He sighed. 'And then, just when we were at our most desperate, she came to us with a bargain – a way to protect what was left. She wanted someone to help her track sky whales, and she had heard about our abilities. The Kotarth leaders decided that I would go with her and help her hunt the creatures we love so much. In return, she promised that my kind, and what was left of our home, would be safe. I worked for her for many, many years and she kept her promise, as did

I, but a time came when I could do it no longer.'

His tail rose, swishing backwards and forwards ferociously.

'I decided that I had to fight back. I joined the Smog Rats as their spy, putting my own life and the lives of my entire race at risk. During this last trip, I knew she was beginning to suspect me, but I was desperate to save this whale while I still could. I took a lot more risks than I would usually, using her radio, causing navigation errors – anything that would give away our position.'

A glimmer in the dark made them both look up as Albi landed on the ship's bow. Where the *Raven* had its harpoon gun, the *Nightjar* had a figurehead instead – a beautiful sculpture of a bird in flight, its head forged in tempered steel and a magnificent plumage of scrap-metal feathers. Albi rested upon its bill and squawked at Katu, who threw him a biscuit.

'The truth is, Miss Starborn, that aboard that ship I was no freer than Albi, locked in that golden cage – her slave, her pet.' Albi caught the biscuit and gobbled it down greedily. 'Now we are both free, soon the sky whale will be also, and freedom is worth more than anything. I think your father was working with us so that, one day, you could be free too.'

Tears flowed down Zeina's face once more. 'What will happen to your home now?' she choked.

'Steele will instruct the mining grounds to advance their machines and my kind will have to choose; they can hide

223

in the forest, until there is nowhere left, or they can fight. But no longer can we save ourselves while Steele and her kind hunt and enslave and pollute everything we hold dear. I have sent them a warning. They know what is coming.'

Katu's head hung low, his tail curled around his legs, his black nose quivered. Zeina shuffled closer and held one of his paws.

'I'm sorry, Katu.'

'I'm sorry too, Miss Starborn. I was suspicious of you from the start. You turned up with what was clearly Smog Rat technology yet seemed to have no idea of the danger. I couldn't work out whether you had been planted by Steele to toy with me, or whether you were a spy or—'

'Just a stupid thief who had no idea that she was putting everyone in danger,' Zeina finished sadly.

'The truth is, we are both guilty of judging the other too harshly.'

They sat like that, hand in paw, for a long time. They sat there until the light of dusk faded altogether, leaving only their gas lamp and the stars. Zeina was beginning to shiver when they heard a commotion coming from the cockpit.

She and Katu found the crew crowded around the radiograph once more, Sparks adjusting wires and turning dials until the gauges sparked to life, needles flickering. Parr was leaning against the wall, arms folded and frowning.

'Zeina!' Jackson cried. 'It's another message!'

Everyone shushed him as a muffled voice came through.

'. . . stranded. Come in, come in . . . *Nightjar*, do you read me?'

Zeina's heart sank; it wasn't her dad, yet the voice sounded familiar somehow.

'Yes. You're coming through now,' shouted Jamie into the receiver. 'Quick, before we lose you again.'

'Scout 2435 reporting . . . We are stranded . . . ship crashed . . . both alive but . . . help.' The message kept fuzzing in and out, but now Zeina knew where she had heard that voice before.

'Is that Shrapnel? It is! That's Shrapnel's voice!' she yelled.

'Sssssshh!' The crowd around the radiograph hushed her and Zeina clapped her hand over her mouth.

'You're coming and going. Try again.' Jamie spoke clearly into the receiver.

'This is Scout 2435 and 9229 . . . In need of urgent assistance . . . Last-known coordinates 27.899 south, 89.788 west . . . alive but . . . need . . . critical . . .'

Fewer and fewer words came through until all that was left was the buzz of the static. Sparks turned the dials but the voice was gone for good. She shrugged at the group surrounding her and then shook her head sadly.

'It's all right, Sparks,' said Jamie. 'You did a good job to get them back at all. Sounds like their radio is pretty damaged.'

'But that was Shrapnel's voice. He's with Dad?' Zeina said, her head swimming once again. She thought about how strangely Shrapnel had acted on the Willoughby Whale. He had seemed so tense and scared for her, quite unlike the adventurous Shrapnel she was used to in Ravenport. He'd warned her about keeping the aerocycle out of sight and she knew that Shrapnel hated many of the Above families – he blamed them for the deaths of his parents, both worked into an early grave by their back-breaking jobs. And yet, somehow, she couldn't imagine her cheerful and carefree friend being serious enough about anything to put his own life at risk. Had her dad asked for his help?

'It sounds like your Shrapnel and our scout 2435 might be the same person too,' Parr sighed.

'We have to find them,' Zeina demanded. 'They're still alive – and now we have their coordinates.' She could have cried with relief.

Parr was silent. She would not look Zeina in the eye.

'Come on! Turn the ship around.'

'They don't know that we have the whale already,' said the captain quietly. 'They don't know that you and Jackson are aboard either. They don't know about what has happened with Steele. She'll have all her short-range airships out looking

for us, not to mention every lawkeeper in a fifty-mile radius –
there's just no way. If they knew, Zeina, they wouldn't ask us
to risk the lives of the whale, of you, or the lives of the crew,
going back for them.'

'You can't just leave them there!' Jackson shouted.
'They'll die!'

'We can try to contact them again, once the whale has
been freed,' Parr said firmly.

'It'll be too late then!' Zeina cried out.

'I'm sorry, Zeina. We would be a sitting target. We haven't
got scout ships. We'd have to lower the *Nightjar* right down
to the ground to get them aboard. There'd be nowhere to
hide and Steele has spies all over the mining grounds.'

Katu spoke up, hands clasped in front of him, his claws
drumming in thought. 'If I may, Captain Parr, I have a
suggestion that would present a lower risk.'

Parr sighed. 'Go on then, Katu.'

'Well, now we know the coordinates, we could fly to that
location but remain hidden in the smog layer, which would
significantly reduce the chance of being spotted. Then Miss
Starborn here, or Master Jackson, who both have experience
flying the aerocycle – well, if they are willing, they could use
it to scout out the exact location of the crash and then, providing
it will take the weight of two, transport the Innovator and the
scout back up to the *Nightjar*, one at a time.'

There was silence as Parr considered this. 'That may well work, but there's still a significant risk of the aerocycle being spotted.'

Zeina nodded. 'Please, Parr? Can we try?'

Parr began to shake her head, but Katu interrupted.

'My calculations suggest that it is worth the risk, Captain Parr. The final decision is yours, of course, but it would be extremely beneficial to have the Innovator safely aboard. He is the only one with the knowledge and experience to make more airships like the *Nightjar.*'

Parr looked down into Zeina's pleading face, still blotchy and red from crying. She was silent for what felt like hours. 'Fine. We can try. But if you or Jackson are found or captured, that's it, we'll have to leave you. Do you understand?'

Zeina nodded, relief flooding through her.

'I'm giving you one hour, that's all. Jamie, tell Beard that we'll need a little extra speed. I really hope I'm not going to regret this!'

CHAPTER 28

The mechanical clanking of the mining grounds echoed the thudding beat of Jackson's heart. An icy wind whipped at his cheeks, forming a maze of frosted crystals around the outer edge of his goggles. He wiped them away, searching the barren, white landscape below. A sharp gust caught him sideways, sending him almost clear off the saddle. The ground seemed to swoop up to meet him at an alarming rate, but he righted himself just in time. Every instinct was telling him to turn around, to get back to the safety of the airship, but he fought on. His arms ached, fingers frozen to the handlebars. His thighs burned. He had been down five times already, as had Zeina, but this was the last try – that's what Parr had said. Their time was almost up and in a matter of minutes the *Nightjar* would start up its engines again, whether he was aboard or not.

Zeina was exhausted. After her last scout, she had collapsed on to the deck, barely able to even hand Jackson the aerocycle. But Jackson knew there was no way she would give in – not until she had found her dad.

Just when it seemed all hope was lost, he saw it; a flickering orange smudge in an otherwise white-grey world. He swooped. Through the flurries of snow and the gloom of the smog, he saw two figures huddled together.

The taller figure spotted him. It shook the smaller one awake and pointed up into the sky. A scorched wreckage of an airship became clear as Jackson nosedived towards them.

'Jackson?' Mr Starborn limped over and enveloped Jackson in the warmest of hugs. 'I don't know . . . how you're here but . . . we are so . . . glad to see you.' His voice was dry and croaked and he let out a rasping cough every few words. Tears welled up in the big man's bloodshot eyes, red-rimmed and burning from having no goggles in the acrid smog.

'There's no time to explain,' Jackson panted. 'Steele's scout ship . . . We've seen it but they haven't spotted us . . . yet. We're up there . . . where the smog is thickest . . . Parr says . . . have to leave soon. Come on . . . have to take both of you.'

'Shrapnel first.' Zeina's dad coughed. 'He's injured and that invention of Zeina's won't hold all three of us.'

Shrapnel objected, but Jackson could see he was in no fit state to wait any longer. He rattled and wheezed, despite having a respirator, and there was a jagged piece of metal sticking out of his left thigh. Shrapnel gasped in agony as Zeina's dad helped him up, pulling and pushing him on to the saddle of the aerocycle. He collapsed heavily against Jackson's back, his arms gripping tightly around his waist. Finally, Mr Starborn wrapped a length of rope around Shrapnel and the saddle to hold him in place and helped him put on a small backpack. 'It's got our supplies in,' he explained, 'and the airship plans. If I don't . . . Well, whatever happens, you give them directly to Captain Parr.'

Jackson didn't waste a second. With a grunt, he pushed off from the ground. The back of the aerocycle swayed and dragged under the extra weight, making it much harder to control against the harsh wind. Pedalling as hard as he could, Jackson set his sights firmly on the ridge where he hoped the *Nightjar* would still be waiting.

Through the railings of the deck, Zeina's anxious face broke into a smile when she saw them. She waved and shouted, running to meet them at the bow.

'Shrapnel! Jackson! Where's Dad? Is he . . . ?'

'He's OK. The ship was just below that last ridge,' Jackson panted back. As his feet touched the planks, he could already hear Parr shouting.

'That's it! No more, Zeina! You've had more than your hour and now Steele's scout knows where we are. Beard, ready the ship for departure. We can't wait any longer.'

Shrapnel was helped off the aerocycle by Jamie, who passed him some goggles. He collapsed on to the deck with a thud, his eyes closing with a flutter. Parr grabbed the front of the aerocycle as Zeina attempted to wrestle it from her.

'My dad is down there!'

'The engines are already going,' Parr said. 'As soon as the ship is ready, we're off. I can't risk the lives of everyone aboard this ship any longer. I'm sorry.'

'Please, just five minutes!'

'You've got three.' Parr let go of the aerocycle with a scowl. 'Any longer and we leave you behind.'

'Fine!' Zeina grabbed the handlebars, but Jackson could see she was still exhausted.

'Let *me* go, Zeina! Come on. I'm faster than you. Three minutes isn't long and I know exactly where to find him too,' Jackson said steadily, keeping his breathing as slow and even as he could. 3.26 minutes happened to be his fastest time on the 1,000-length time-trial track. To get to Mr Starborn and back was at least that distance. He was faster on the aerocycle than his velocycle, he was sure, but then he had to account for stopping to get Zeina's dad, and the extra weight on the way back. He made a mental note to complete some aerocycle time trials of his own if he made it back safely to the *Nightjar*.

'No, I can do it! He's *my* dad!'

'You're exhausted, Zeina. Trust me, OK?'

Some of the tension went out of Zeina's face, her hands giving up their urgent tugging of the handlebars.

'Just promise me you'll be back in time.'

'I promise,' said Jackson as firmly as he could.

She hugged him tightly, hung her respirator around his neck for her dad and Jackson kicked off from the deck, disappearing into the smog.

CHAPTER 29

econds seemed like hours. The whirr of the *Nightjar*'s propellers grew louder. The crew began to shout to one another as they prepared for take-off. Three minutes had passed. The airship rose higher into the air.

'Please, Parr, just a minute more!' The only thing worse than losing her dad, leaving him in the Western Mountains for ever, would be to lose both him and Jackson all at once. It was unimaginable.

'We can't wait, Zeina!'

Zeina's eyes searched the smog for any sign of the aerocycle. Her hands shook; her heart pounded.

The *Nightjar* began to gain height and turned, setting off west. Zeina ran to the ship's stern and hung over the railings, waving and shouting into the smog.

'Jackson! We're here! Come on!'

'Quiet, Zeina! You'll alert every lawkeeper for miles,' Parr shouted back from the bridge.

'Look!' Shrapnel was pointing from the starboard side. 'That's got to be them!'

There was a dark blur in the smog, moving at speed towards them. Rapidly, the shadow became more defined, and Zeina's heart skipped as she made out the two figures clinging on to the aerocycle. They were travelling fast – far too fast . . .

With an almighty bang, the aerocycle crashed into the *Nightjar*'s deck, causing the whale to moan and smack its tail against the wood. Jackson, her dad and the aerocycle lay in a heap upon the decking, heads and arms, and legs and wheels, and metal and pedals, all twisted around each other – battered, bruised and bent out of shape, but alive, and that was all that mattered.

Zeina launched herself at the pair. Jackson let out an "OOOF" as she landed heavily on top of them, her arms reaching around their necks and pinning them to the deck.

'Give them some room,' Jamie laughed, hauling her up.

Jackson managed to untangle himself first. He had scrapes and grazes from the landing, but seemed otherwise unharmed. She grabbed him in a hug, placing a rough kiss on his non-grazed cheek.

'Thank you, Jackson! I knew you could do it.' They both knew, strictly speaking, this was untrue but nevertheless Jackson's cheeks burned a happy crimson.

'Dad!' Zeina held out her hand, which he gripped tightly.

'Zeina,' he rasped, tears clouding his goggles.

He was unable to stand without the help of both Zeina and Jamie. Together, they helped him limp below deck. Zeina watched as Jamie checked her dad over. His hand and wrist were roughly bandaged in a rag, stiff with brown blood. He winced as Jamie took it off to examine his arm. Releasing him from his respirator and goggles, Zeina noticed his lip was split, purple and oozing, and his right eye so bruised that it had swollen shut. One ankle bulged unnaturally, covered in blue-green smudges, and the crash-landing on the deck had caused a fresh red cut down one knee.

Zeina quivered with impatience until Jamie finally gave her the all-clear and she could hurl herself into her father's arms.

'I'm so sorry, Dad,' Zeina sobbed. 'I shouldn't have left like that. It's my fault. It's all my fault.'

'Oh, Zeina,' he said. 'It's my fault, not yours. I never should have tried to hide so much from you.' He unfurled her from his arms, his one non-swollen eye twinkling mischievously. 'Though some of it actually *is* your fault. The – what did Jackson call it? – the *aerocycle*, for example. Not to mention joining a dangerous mission to catch a sky whale without asking me. But let's not dwell on those for now, eh?'

'Hey, without the aerocycle you'd still be stuck down there on that ridge!'

He laughed, and so did she, and then they were both laughing and crying and hugging.

'Why didn't you tell me about the Smog Rats? I could have helped.'

'Oh, I don't know' he sighed sadly. 'Now I wish more than anything that I had.'

'You didn't trust me?'

He put his arm round her. 'No, Zeina. That's not it. I wanted to, but I also just wanted you to be free from all this for a little bit longer. You're still so young.'

From the inside pocket of his jacket, he took out a picture. It was one Zeina had seen many times before – a tiny square scrap, its edges white and peeling, showing her and her mum when she was just a baby.

'You are so much like her,' her dad said, taming a stray curl by brushing it gently behind her ear. 'You know that we met on an airship? One I was repairing back when I first started working for Jackson's grandad. She was an engine-room worker – she loved the adventure of airship travel but the work was so hard and she had to give it up when she got pregnant with you.'

Tears spilled down his cheeks and his voice began to break.

'I always suspected she did some scouting for the Smog Rats. She was good friends with Shrapnel's parents; they all worked in the engine room together. She'd never said for certain but then, after you were born, she told me – said she needed to do one last job and then she'd give it up for ever.'

Zeina's chest tightened. Her mum had been a Smog Rat? 'I didn't even know the Smog Rats had been around that long.'

'For as long as there have been sky whale hotels, there have been people trying to stop them. Back then, the Smog Rats were an extensive network of unregistered airships that targeted the sky whale hunters. But the lawmakers were making it harder and harder for them to buy ore, forcing them underground. Your mum asked me to make an airship part from some unfinished plans – their Innovator had been killed. It was a small chamber that burned smog instead of ore, a prototype.'

'Like the part I stole for the aerocycle?'

'That's right. I made it as best I could, and she promised that delivering it would be the last job she'd do. She set off but never returned. They . . . they always said the airship crash was an accident. But I was never sure.' He wiped away tears and sniffed. 'I remember looking at you, so small and helpless, and vowing to keep you out of all that – no airship travel, no Smog Rats. And for ten years, I did just that. The Smog Rats were all but disappearing and it was easy to pretend they didn't exist at all.'

'What changed your mind?' asked Zeina.

'You did,' he smiled, stroking away her tears with his

non-bandaged hand. 'You grew up to be so like your mum, yearning for adventure, to explore and change the world. I knew you would never be happy staying in Ravenport. And so, two years ago, when Shrapnel's dad came to me and asked for my help, I couldn't say no. I began work on the plans for the *Nightjar*. I made a new prototype chamber and tested it until I was sure it would work on a larger scale. When his dad died, Shrapnel took over from him as my scout. He acted as my go-between – sending messages, plans and parts between me and Captain Parr, who bit-by-bit built the *Nightjar* in secret in the north.' He paused as Shrapnel's raised voice could be heard – Jamie was obviously trying to remove the metal from his leg. 'I wonder what Shrapnel's father would say to me now. I don't think he'd ever imagined that I'd get his son this far in. We're all outlaws now. None of us can ever go back.'

CHAPTER 30

Shrapnel was crying out in pain. It had taken Jamie a while to extract the shard of metal, which now lay on the deck sticky with congealing globules of red. Jackson winced, looking away while he picked it up gingerly.

'What are you doing?' Shrapnel asked through clenched teeth. He wriggled and writhed as Jamie attempted to stitch up the deep red gash on his thigh.

'Er . . . I thought I'd get rid of it?' Jackson replied.

'Er, no thanks!' replied Shrapnel, snatching it away from Jackson and placing it lovingly on his chest. 'I'm keeping this as a souvenir!'

Why anyone would want a souvenir of this particular moment, Jackson could not fathom. He was sure he heard a little almost-giggle from Sparks, who hovered nearby passing Jamie needles and thread. She did not seem to be at all afraid of Shrapnel, despite the blood and the howling racket he was making with every new stitch; there was nothing to give him to ease the pain.

'Need a rest? We can take a little break?' Jamie asked.

'No! Please! Let's just get it over with!'

Sparks held out her hand for Shrapnel's.

'Oh yeah, like that is going to help.' He rolled his eyes, but took it nevertheless, giving her a little wink.

The baby whale began to bang its tail noisily on the deck. Its flippers flashed and beat against the net, making the airship wobble.

'Jackson? Try to keep him calm, will you?' said Jamie. 'I'll be finished here in a minute.'

Jackson opened another disgusting bottle of fishy gruel. The whale opened its mouth to reveal its huge teeth and a spongey pink tongue. Jackson gulped but patted the whale on the temple with his free hand and it grunted appreciatively.

'Looks like you have a new friend there, Master Willoughby, if I may say so, that is, sir?' Shrapnel said in mock formality. He attempted to salute but Jamie had stuck his needle in and this caused Shrapnel to cry out again instead.

'I'm not a Willoughby anymore, Shrapnel, just Jackson.' Since coming aboard the *Nightjar*, Jackson had worked hard to leave all that behind him. He was enjoying feeling like one of a team for the first time in his life and Shrapnel, with his constant teasing, was ruining all that.

'Oh, I do apologise, Master Jackson,' said Shrapnel with another wink at Sparks. 'I will make sure I—Ow!'

Zeina and her father emerged from the cabins, red-eyed but smiling. Her dad went to find Captain Parr on the bridge but Zeina ran to Shrapnel and gave him the biggest hug.

'Ah! Get off, Zee!' Shrapnel laughed, elbowing her away. 'Can't you see I'm busy here?'

'I'm so glad you're all right,' she beamed, ruffling his head affectionately. 'You'd better hurry up and get your leg fixed up – we're full-time Smog Rats now and there'll be plenty of work for you to do as soon as you're better.'

Jackson watched from the sidelines, feeling as if he wasn't there at all and wondering if Zeina would ever need his help again.

CHAPTER 31

'Nice work, Zeina. Now, if I pass you the sheet metal, do you think you can secure it over the hole?'

Zeina pedalled frantically to keep up with the *Nightjar*. Despite his bandaged hand, it had taken her dad no time at all to fix up her aerocycle and, together, they were attempting to repair the hole in the smog chamber left by the harpoon. Zeina held the aerocycle steady with her knees and reached out for the metal her dad passed her. One hand held it in place over the break in the hull, while the other grabbed bolts and tools from a belt slung around her middle.

'That's it! Try not to get right in front of the smoke – it's smog from the chamber that hasn't been burnt up yet. Perfect.'

Zeina felt so happy to be working alongside her dad once more. She hadn't realised quite how much she had missed it until this moment. He waved her back in, smiling despite his swollen eye.

They were above the cloud layer once again. The echoed

blasts and clanking machinery were getting quieter and less frequent, and the smell of burning rocks was gradually being replaced by a breeze with a woody freshness to it. Jackson and Jamie were tending to the baby whale, which was becoming more and more fractious as the sedative wore off, and Shrapnel – leg stitched and bandaged – was curled up, having a nap after his ordeal.

'That's it, Parr,' her dad called down to the bridge. 'She's patched up and ready to go, if you want to increase speed.'

'Great! How much longer, Katu?' Captain Parr shouted up to the crow's nest.

'Another mile or two and then we can descend,' Katu yelled back, standing statue-still as he always did when he was tracking something. 'The pod is nearby – I can sense it. We should go below the cloud layer soon. Don't want to come down right on top of them. They will attack if they think we are keeping the baby . . .' His voice trailed off.

'Katu?' Parr called up again.

Katu was silent for a moment and Zeina knew that if she could see him, his eyes would be closed, ears pricked up, fur standing up on end.

'Something else is coming. Behind us and quickly. It's another airship!' He grabbed his spyglass, zooming in on a tiny spot off the starboard side, hovering just under the clouds. 'It's the *Raven*!'

'I knew it wouldn't be too long. Starborn, can we increase speed any further? Will the hull hold up? We don't want them to get within harpoon range.'

'Ready to go, Captain,' Zeina's dad replied.

'Beard? Where are you?'

'I'm here, Penny!' His cheeky face poked up from below deck.

'It's Captain Parr to you and get a move on! We need full capacity if we're going to stay out of range.'

'Right you are. We're on it!'

The loud whirring of the cycle-powered generators started up once again and the airship leapt forward. The whale thrashed against its net and hammered the deck with its tail, lumina lines flashing more and more vividly as they grew closer to the pod.

'Can't release it yet,' said Jamie. 'We need to be in sight of the pod.'

There was a roar from behind them and the *Raven* rose out of the cloud layer, funnels billowing thick black smoke, pistons groaning. They were a way off, but if she squinted, Zeina could make out the silhouette of Steele in her furs, standing on the bow of the ship next to the harpoon gun, spyglass in hand. She was waving one of the dart guns in the air and shouting something that Zeina couldn't quite make out. Her crew laughed triumphantly.

'Below the clouds! Quickly!' shouted Parr. 'There's no hiding for us now, but we need to release the whale before they have a chance to dart and recapture it.'

The *Nightjar* plunged downwards into the clouds and everything went white. Everyone Zeina cared about in the whole world was aboard this airship and imagining what could happen to them all was terrifying.

CHAPTER 32

The thick green canopy of Howlingwood soon came into view. Katu was right, the pod wasn't too far off and they seemed much more agitated than they had before the whale hunt. Adults and young alike propelled themselves this way and that, frustrated, as if they were searching for something they couldn't find. Their lumina lines burned with an angry glow.

'A little closer but that's all. They'll attack the airship if they think we want to harm the babies,' yelled Parr. 'Jamie, start loosening the net as best you can. Get that little one ready to go.'

'On it, Captain!' he shouted back, beckoning Jackson over. 'Come on, lad, he likes you. You can help me release him.'

Jackson approached the thrashing whale with trepidation.

'Won't he . . . attack us, maybe? After we let him go?'

'There's always that possibility,' said Jamie, not looking concerned in the least. 'But it's unlikely. He should see the pod and be more worried about getting back to his mummy. Try to keep him calm and I'll get round and loosen all the fastenings.'

Jackson gulped but gave the whale a reassuring rub on the back.

There was another roar behind them as the *Raven* plunged through the cloud layer. The crew were still laughing and they were so close now that Jackson could make out the words Steele was shouting to her crew.

'I'll give a month's wages to anyone who can dart the Willoughby boy, and two if you get that sneaky, spying cat!'

'Hold on, everyone!' yelled Parr. 'We're almost in range of their harpoon. Jamie, release the whale! We need to get out of here now!'

'You ready, lad?' Jamie asked Jackson. 'Hold that pulley steady and I'll do this one. We pull up on the count of three and that will release him from the net. Stand back, everyone!'

Everything seemed to happen at once. As Jamie counted, 'ONE ... TWO ... THREE!' Jackson also heard Steele yell 'FIRE!' from behind them. Her voice carried clearly on the wind; it sounded as if she was standing on the deck of the *Nightjar* itself. There was a loud BANG, BANG, SMASH on the deck as the whale pummelled it with its newly freed tail, making a large hole in the planks. At the same time, there was a WHOOSH of metal cutting through air; the *Raven* had fired their harpoon. Parr swerved the *Nightjar* sharply over to starboard and the harpoon missed their hull by centimetres.

'Reload! We'll get them next time!' called out Vivianne to raucous cheers from the crew. There were several smaller whooshes and Katu was forced to duck and hide as whaling darts flew at his shoulders and ears.

'Where in heavens is the whale?' shouted Parr. Jackson had expected to see it shoot off in front of them as soon as it was released but, now the *Nightjar* had righted itself again, the whale was nowhere to be seen. 'It can't have just disappeared,' Parr yelled. 'It's a flippin' whale!'

'Look over the railings, Captain. He's been scared by that harpoon strike.'

Zeina and Jackson rushed over to the railings and hung over the edge. Sure enough, Jackson could see two great flippers sweeping out from under the airship's hull. The whale roared and struck the hull with its tail, making the airship jolt upwards suddenly. It tried to fly out but – WHOOSH! – another harpoon sailed past, narrowly missing the whale and causing it to dash back to safety underneath the airship.

'We have to get it to move!' yelled Parr. 'What is it doing, Jamie?'

'It's got confused. It can't work out how to get back to the pod safely.'

'We're going to have to change course soon, or we'll end up right in the pod ourselves. We're sitting ducks for that harpoon! It has to leave us now so that we can try and divert them away from it.'

The *Raven* was now so close that bullets from their pistols were reaching the stern. They clattered off the metal and flew over the railings. The Smog Rats ducked and then fired their own pistols back towards Steele's crew.

Shrapnel had pulled himself up on the railings, watching the whale with Zeina and Jackson. In a flurry of white, a little hand grasped Shrapnel's. With a desperate tug on his sleeve, he bent down, craning to hear what Sparks had to say to him above the noisy chaos surrounding them. She got her mouth right up close to his ear and whispered.

'Hey!' Shrapnel shouted. 'I think Sparks has an idea. She said something to me but it doesn't make any sense!'

'What was it?' asked Zeina, ducking a bullet that zoomed past her head.

'She said . . . Fish guts?'

'Fish guts?!'

'Fish guts? That was it, wasn't it?' Shrapnel asked Sparks, who smiled and nodded vigorously.

'That doesn't make any sense,' cried Zeina. Sparks frowned at her and folded her skinny little arms over her chest.

Jackson gasped, an idea – Sparks's idea – becoming clear

in his mind. 'Yes, it does! Quick, Zeina, where's your aerocycle? I think this might just work.'

He ran back to Jamie, grabbing two bottles of murky brown water as Zeina went to fetch the aerocycle.

'Right! Now, get on the back and I'll do the pedalling,' he said, emptying out one bottle of the brown whale fish-gut food over her head and the other over himself.

'Argh! What is this stuff?' She retched, holding her hand over her mouth. Murky liquid dripped down her face and fish parts stuck to her hair and nose. 'Argh! It stinks!'

'It's fish guts! And that's the point! Come on! The whale will follow us and we can lead it in the right direction until it spots the pod.'

Sparks smiled, looking at Jackson with a new-found appreciation.

'Wait!' yelled Zeina's dad, hurrying over to them. 'What are you doing? You can't fly that thing here! There are harpoons and darts flying around, not to mention a pod of sky whales. It's just too dangerous. Here, I'll do it!'

'Dad, you've only got one good eye, not to mention your hand! Plus Jackson is by far the fastest on the aerocycle. He can fly and I can be lookout. We know it can support two people. Me and Jackson are a great team. Let us try!'

Jackson's heart swelled. He wasn't certain the plan would work but this was something he could do, something he was better at than anyone on the ship and, despite his fear, Zeina's faith in them made him feel brave.

'You're not going.' Mr Starborn gripped the aerocycle's handlebars firmly.

'Dad, if we don't try, then we're all done for anyway!' The ship veered and jolted as another harpoon was fired. This one narrowly missed the port side.

'Come on, they're getting closer and we can't speed up anymore. It's the only way, Dad!'

Mr Starborn groaned but let go of the aerocycle and helped Jackson on to the saddle. He went to kiss Zeina's forehead, but, smelling the brown, putrid liquid glooping down from her hair, decided it was best not to and hugged her gingerly instead. He carefully embraced Jackson too and with a pat on his back, they were off.

CHAPTER 33

At first, Zeina thought Sparks's plan had failed miserably. They flew off, weaving and swerving to avoid darts, but the whale didn't follow them. It stayed beneath the airship, flying forward a little before more darts were fired and it retreated.

Then there was a gust of wind. It rustled through the trees, making them howl in agony. Zeina and Jackson would have been knocked off the aerocycle completely were it not for Jackson's flying. He darted and dived, correcting the aerocycle quickly with Zeina's arms clenched tightly around his waist. She looked behind them. They were out of range of Steele's dart guns now.

'Ah, Jackson? You might want to speed up a bit.'

'Why, is it working?' He started to turn his head but Zeina stopped him.

'No, I'll look! You concentrate on flying. Let's just say, I think he's caught our scent!'

The baby whale had accelerated out from under the *Nightjar* and was flying straight for them, its huge mouth wide open. She could see three rows of jagged teeth and a wide, rubbery pink tongue.

'Jackson! Can't we go any faster?'

'We can but we're almost at the pod! He needs to realise that quickly or we'll end up as whale food.'

The aerocycle sped up further, wind whipping at their sopping-wet clothes. Jackson skilfully changed direction, heading up then down, turning right then left, in a desperate attempt to shake the baby whale off their track.

Zeina peeped behind them again. The whale was very close, its mouth gaping open. It was going to swallow them whole!

She saw the *Nightjar* turn steeply upwards into the cloud layer and disappear. 'They're leaving us,' she yelled to Jackson over the baying wind. 'The *Nightjar* has gone!'

'They'll be trying to divert the *Raven* away from us,' Jackson shouted back.

But the *Raven* didn't follow the *Nightjar* towards the cloud layer; they increased their speed, focusing instead on Jackson, Zeina and the whale. The aerocycle was now going so fast that Zeina had to have one arm hooked around Jackson's chest at all times. The other gripped the back of the saddle so she could still turn and see what was going on behind them.

There was an eerie howl from the forest below as another gust of wind knocked them sideways. The whale was just metres away now, its mouth even wider and lumina lines flashing wildly. It let out a low moaning growl that startled Jackson, making him turn his head.

'Don't look! Just keep pedalling!' she shouted, feeling his heart jump and flutter behind his ribs.

'Zeina! He's going to eat us!'

Jackson drove the aerocycle down towards the trees and then up and sharply right, trying desperately to shake him off, but the whale followed, closer than ever. A film of saliva coated each shining white tooth and its wet tongue was covered in bumps and grooves.

'I'm sorry, Zeina. This was a stupid idea.' Jackson was faltering, his foot missed a pedal and the aerocycle fell a few metres.

'Keep going!' Zeina yelled. There was another low growl, so loud and so close that Zeina could feel the warmth of the whale's breath. Big wet globules of whale spit splashed her back and neck. The children clung to each other, eyes squeezed shut, knees gripping the aerocycle. There was a roar behind them, and then a blast of air above their heads sent them into a steep nosedive. Jackson clutched the handlebars tightly and Zeina gripped his waist, hiding her face in his back. She waited for the warm wet breath to consume them, but it never came.

'Zeina! It's seen them!'

The blast of air was an almighty swish from the baby whale's tail above their heads. At last, it had spotted its pod and given up on its meal, sailing over Jackson and Zeina. The adults had spotted it too and were flying towards it.

'Quick!' said Zeina. 'Up to the cloud layer before they decide they fancy a little reunion snack!'

They soared upwards, Zeina turning back to watch the whale's progress.

'Will it make it?' asked Jackson. 'Will the *Raven* catch it?'

But the *Raven* looked as if it had, at last, given up on the whale. As soon as Jackson had started flying up, it too changed its direction. Darts flew at Zeina's and Jackson's heads as they dodged and swerved.

'Ready the harpoon!' Zeina heard Vivianne's voice clearly on the wind. It was determined, unflinching and made Zeina's blood run cold.

'At the children, mistress?'

'Yes, Boris! At the children! I swear if you miss this time, I'll feed you to that whale pod myself.'

Zeina saw the figure of Boris at the ship's bow, his arm resting on the lever of the harpoon gun. Its pointed blade gleamed in the sunlight. The *Raven* seemed closer than ever as Zeina heard Steele begin her countdown.

'THREE!' The aerocycle weaved closer and closer to the

cloud layer, Jackson panting and pedalling with all his remaining energy.

'TWO!' The *Raven* roared behind them, a plume of smoke choking from its funnels.

'ONE!' Zeina stared at the cloud layer, just metres away from them now.

'FI—Ahhh!'

A high, terrified shriek from Steele made Zeina turn. Vivianne was huddled in a ball on the deck, both arms flung over her head in an attempt to protect her face, a deep red gash across one of her hands. A flapping, croaking, hissing, scratching bird was trying desperately to attack her face, white claws bared angrily, his beak pecking and pulling at her hair. Albi's wings beat furiously at his old mistress as he snapped at her amber locks, pulling them out in great clumps with his feet.

'Get the children! Fire!' Steele yelled as she tried to fight Albi off.

But at that moment Boris, Steele and everyone else aboard the *Raven* were knocked clean off their feet as an enormous adult sky whale slammed into the ship from below. The *Raven* was thrown up into the air and then fell from the sky, careering down towards the forest at a tremendous speed, tumbling and turning, its stern smashed, its hull broken clean in two. The whale chased it down, ripping at the ship with its jaws. Steele's eyes were wide with surprise and fear as she clung desperately to the railings.

CRASH! Zeina watched as the bow of the famous airship slammed into the treetops and was consumed completely by the dark forest. SMASH! The stern, with its billowing funnels, followed it, breaking into pieces on impact. There was an almighty explosion and then a column of thick black smoke emerged from the dense trees of Howlingwood.

CHAPTER 34

Everyone aboard the *Nightjar* had been kept very busy since the airship battle over Howlingwood. Sometimes Jackson helped Zeina and her dad with their engineering jobs – Parr had them improving the smog chamber as well as developing and building more aerocycles – but he was much more suited to navigation duty.

Most of his time was spent in the cockpit with Captain Parr, or up in the crow's nest with Katu and Albi. Jackson had learned more from them in the past weeks than in all of his hours of lessons with his tutor back in Ravenport. When there wasn't work to do, he and Zeina would sneak off and train on the aerocycle – she wanted to be just as fast as he was. Even Shrapnel seemed to have a new-found respect for Jackson since the rescue of the baby whale. He still joked and messed with him in a way that irritated Jackson enormously. But he had also asked Jackson to help him learn how to fly the aerocycle as soon as his leg was better, and Jackson thought that they could maybe become friends.

The *Nightjar* was taking the slow route back east, going around the Northern Mountains in order to stay out of sight. They had contacts in the north too, where fresh supplies and parts could be picked up. Life seemed peaceful and happy. However, Jackson knew that he had a decision to make and that soon the time would come when he could avoid it no longer.

'We'll be back over the Eastern Continent in a couple of days,' said Parr, showing Jackson their position on the map. 'Soon we'll have to go back into the smog layer during the day and do most of our long-distance flying at night. We've got a message to one of our scouts down there and she's picked up a few more of the parts Starborn asked for, as well as some other supplies for Jamie.'

Parr looked very hard at him with her good eye. 'Now's the time to make up your mind, Jackson. If you want to go back, you can. Our scout can get you to the nearest town. If you tell them who you are and say you don't remember what happened or how you got there, they'll get you back to Ravenport before your "funeral". You'd have your inheritance – there'd be nothing Hamilton could do to stop you. You could take over the Willoughby Whale and chuck out your awful uncle and cousin or you could go to the next Ravenport Racer trials. You'd be a shoo-in, all the practice you've had recently on the aerocycle.'

Jackson didn't answer. How he would love to turn up and wipe that awful smugness off Hamilton's face. He considered his parents, who never really cared about him but still shouldn't have died the way they did. He remembered his enormous apartment in Willoughby Towers, his velocycle collection and Flora's delicious cooking. He thought of Franklyn Beaumont and the looks on the faces of his team in that victorious photo when they won the cup.

'The thing is, if you choose to stay, that's it. Next week we get back to our primary objective – freeing sky whales, raiding the Above whale hotels. You won't ever be able to go back to your old life. You'll be an outlaw, just like the rest of us.'

Jackson frowned. Going back would mean having anything money could buy – the newest velocycle models, mountains of delicious food, fancy parties, enormous gifts, servants and a wardrobe full of luxurious clothes. He could join the velocycle team, have teammates and victories, maybe even crowds asking him for his autograph. He could get his revenge on Hamilton – cut off his money and throw him and Herbert out of their home. But did any of that really compete with what he had now? Being part of the *Nightjar* crew, being with Zeina, learning about the four continents from a real captain? And could he even go back to his old lifestyle knowing all the misery his family had caused in order to achieve it? The last month had changed him completely and yet made him feel more himself than he ever had.

'If I stay, we can still punish Hamilton somehow, can't we? We can try to stop him and Herbert from doing any more harm?'

'Course, lad! We'd be doing that whether you were to stay with us or not.'

'I'd like to stay here with you then, if that's OK, Parr?'

She looked stern. 'You're sure? You'll have to work hard for everything you get and it'll be dangerous work – there's the distinct chance we'll all end up dead or in the mining grounds.'

'This is where I'd like to be. If that's all right with you?' he replied nervously.

She beamed and patted him roughly on the back. 'Of course it is, lad! We'll be happy to have you! Now, up to that crow's nest and give Katu a hand.'

CHAPTER 35

Zeina was hammering nails into the freshly painted wooden planks of the *Nightjar*'s deck. Her dad always seemed to have an endless list of jobs for her to do and, today, Zeina was feeling particularly hard done by, as it was her birthday. If she had been back at home in Ravenport, they would have had a little party – something to celebrate beginning her apprenticeship and never having to go back to that stuffy school again. She would have had a cake, a few gifts and she was sure her dad would have given her the day off from airship duties.

There was no such luck now she and her father were outlaws – official members of the *Nightjar* Smog Rats. It seemed her dad had still not quite forgiven her for the danger she had managed to get herself into, judging by the huge number of menial jobs he asked her to do.

The *Nightjar* was almost completely repaired from its battle with the *Raven* and now it was all hands to the pump in order to prepare the ship to set off into the Eastern Continent again. The ship was currently making the most of its last breaths of clear atmosphere, coasting just beyond the puffed white clouds of the Northern Mountains. The sun beat down upon the deck, making Zeina sweat and huff.

'Are you absolutely sure you got all those fish guts off you?' teased Shrapnel, nostrils flaring in disgust. He was watching her from a deck chair, his bad leg raised up. 'I'm sure I keep getting a whiff of something when the sun shines on you.'

Zeina resisted the temptation to throw her hammer at him. 'You could always come and help, you know? We would get it done in half the time and then you could watch me test the new aerocycle.'

'I'd love to, Zee, but Jamie says I need to rest if I'm going to heal. A day or two more of sitting here in the sunshine should do it.' He smiled and rattled his canteen. 'Any chance of a refill?'

Zeina snorted. 'Get it yourself, lazy! You've got your crutches.'

Jamie had fashioned Shrapnel some crutches out of a mop handle, a walking stick, a sponge and a cushion. However, before Shrapnel could even think about getting up, there was Sparks with a freshly filled canteen for him. She often appeared like that, as if from nowhere, and Zeina had come to understand that wherever you were on the ship, it was best just to assume Sparks was somewhere nearby, watching and listening.

'Oh, thank you, Sparks. See, Zeina – someone knows how to treat a patient round here.'

Sparks blushed and ran off happily.

'And what exactly is your job going to be once you can work like the rest of us?' Zeina asked Shrapnel.

'Oh, I don't know. What does Jackson do? Rich boys don't know anything about working airships.'

'Parr manages to keep Jackson busy, don't you worry!'

'That's if he chooses to stay . . .' Shrapnel said slyly.

Yes, if he chooses to stay, Zeina thought miserably to herself. She couldn't bear the alternative, but there was Willoughby Towers, his fortune, the Ravenport Racers and the chance to punish Hamilton to compete with. Who would give up all that? She bit her lip and concentrated hard on the deck. She knew Jackson had to make his decision soon and was desperate to ask him, yet she was terrified it would not be the answer she hoped for.

'Well,' continued Shrapnel, 'my skills mostly involve shovelling ore and there's not much use for that on this ship. I'm sure Parr will find a use for me somewhere.'

After the deck was finished, Zeina took her chance. Looking around to check that her dad was nowhere in sight, she sneaked up to the crow's nest. Katu was at his post, spyglass in hand and Albi happily perched upon his shoulder.

'Ah ha, Miss Zeina,' he said without looking round. 'Escaping from your work duties, I see.'

'It is my birthday, Katu. Don't Kotarth get days off for their birthdays?'

'The Kotarth do not celebrate such things as birthdays, Miss Zeina. Our celebrations revolve around group achievements rather than the selfish celebrations of individuals.'

'Oh.'

By now Zeina was used to Katu's bluntness. She quite liked his straightforward way of talking, even if it sometimes sounded a little rude to humans.

'Have you decided if you are going to stay with us, Katu?' she asked hopefully. Now she had befriended the Kotarth, she could not bear the thought of losing him as well as Jackson.

'I will remain here for now,' he replied. 'I must atone for the hurt I have caused our beloved sky whales in recent years. There will be time enough later for me to return to my family and forest.'

'Oh, Katu! That's great news!' She launched herself at him and put her arms around his furry middle.

The sound of feet climbing the rungs up to the crow's nest made her release him. She turned to see Jackson clambering through the hatch.

266

'Hello, Katu. Zeina! I was hoping you'd be up here too.'

'Ssssssssh!' Zeina said in a hushed whisper. 'My dad doesn't know I'm here!'

'OK, well, I have some—'

Jackson was interrupted by the sound of Zeina's dad, his voice floating up from somewhere below.

'Zeina? Are you up there?'

'Oh no!' Zeina went to call back down but was stopped by Katu.

'How about I tell your dad I saw you head down to check on the cycle generators? That should give you at least five more minutes. It is your birthday, after all,' Katu said, golden eyes aglow as he descended the ladder.

'What was it that you wanted to say?' Zeina asked Jackson once Katu had gone. She wasn't sure she could hear it – not like this, not just the two of them – and then pretend that she was happy for him. He looked nervous; his skin had that sweaty pallor she had seen so much of during the first days of their trip and his eyes were huge and round. She knew in her heart what was coming.

'Well, I've decided to stay here . . . with you . . . I mean, with all of you. I'm not going back to Ravenport.' It came out all at once, in a garbled mess, and it took Zeina a second or two to comprehend what he was saying.

'Oh, Jackson!' she shouted despite herself, and flung her

arms around his neck. 'I can't believe it! I felt sure you were going to choose to go home.'

'You're not disappointed?'

She punched him in the ribs, laughing. 'Of course not, you idiot! I've been so worried you wouldn't stay. This is the best birthday present I could have asked for.' She hugged him again, making him blush to the very tips of his ears.

'Zeina?' Her shout had given her away and now there was no hiding. 'Come on down. Jackson, you too!'

'Oh no,' hissed Zeina. 'OK, Dad,' she yelled. 'I'll be down in a minute!' She released Jackson. 'You're sure, aren't you? You won't change your mind?'

'I've never been so certain about anything,' he said.

Zeina beamed. 'Come on, let's go down and tell Dad. Shrapnel too – he'll be so pleased!'

'Really?' wondered Jackson.

'He quite likes you now, I think . . .' She clambered down the ladder excitedly, a great weight lifted from her.

When they arrived, her dad and Parr were deep in conversation with Katu. Captain Parr's eyes lit up when she saw them both. 'Ah! Jackson, it seems you made your decision just in time. We've had a radio message.'

'Who from?' Jackson asked.

'It's from our scout – she's got our supplies but she also had news for us. There's a whale hotel making its way north

268

from the eastern cruising circuit. In a few days from now, it will be in perfect position – isolated from the tourist route and easy for us to reach. So I suppose what I'm really saying is, are you both ready for your first raid?'

They turned to look at each other, Zeina flushed with excitement and Jackson pale with nerves. Yet each knew that with the other there beside them, they were ready for anything. Zeina grinned.

EPILOGUE

RUTHLESS RATS RANSACK WILLOUGHBY WHALE

After the recent and dramatic increase in attacks by the so-called Smog Rat pirates, yesterday was the turn of the Willoughby Whale, the largest and most luxurious hotel in the Eastern Continent. Reports suggest that the ruthless attack began at around 2 a.m., while guests slept soundly in their beds.

'There just was no warning!' said Nelly Upton, an engine room worker onboard on the night of the attack. 'First thing we knew was the alarm going off. Ship didn't make a sound!'

After stealing and vandalising property, the Rats attacked the STAN system, which caused the terrified and confused whale to panic and ascend above the limit of the Upper Atmosphere. Sky whale biologists working for the Willoughby family are concerned about the whale's health.

'It is the oldest of the whale hotels,' explained Beau Moreton, a STANS room scientist who narrowly escaped with her life. 'We are not sure how long it will last without us there to love and care for it.'

Fortunately, due to the heroic acts of our ever vigilant and honourable lawkeepers, there were no human fatalities. After the alarm was raised, guests and staff were quickly loaded on to short-range life-ships and transported safely back to Ravenport. However, a number of exhibits from Ravenport Zoo were also onboard the whale, animals rescued by selfless entrepreneur and owner of the Willoughby Whale, Hamilton Willoughby. The whereabouts and safety of these vulnerable beasts remain unknown.

Mr Willoughby was kind enough to provide us with a statement at this difficult time. 'Truly, we are shocked and dismayed. I was so concerned about the safety of my guests and staff that I refused to leave until everyone else was safe. Indeed, I narrowly made it out with my life! Some of my most gracious friends have suggested I deserve a medal for my courage, but I will not hear of it. Thinking of others

271

comes naturally to me and I did only what anyone would have done. This evil attack comes at a particularly sad time for the Willoughby family. We are still very much mourning the sad loss of my brother and sister-in-law, followed by the horrific death of my dearest nephew. Smog Rats were implicated in both these incidents and I can see no reason for the Willoughby family to have been so cruelly targeted. It is a dangerous time for us all and I believe all Above families must come together to protect ourselves and, of course, the Belows that rely on us. Lawmakers must make every effort to find these fiends quickly and give them the harshest of punishments. A life sentence in the mining grounds is too good for them!'

This is the third attack on a whale hotel in recent weeks and comes only a month after brave and beloved explorer, Vivianne Steele, and her legendary airship, the *Raven,* were ambushed by the same band of pirates and tragically crashed on the Western Continent. The whereabouts and well-being of Miss Steele and her crew remain unknown as all attempts to recover the wreckage have been thwarted by the recent Kotarth uprising in the region.

It is feared by some that the Smog Rats may have

a network of spies working within our towns and cities and onboard our airships and whale hotels. Lawmakers have promised to train thousands more lawkeepers and give them new powers to arrest and detain suspects. They have also increased checks at ore refuelling stations and increased punishments for anyone supplying unregistered airships with fuel.

'This will not be the end for the Willoughby Whale,' announced Hamilton Willoughby at the close of his press conference yesterday. 'We will not be beaten! Already, I have plans to capture a new whale and build the greatest and most magnificent whale hotel the four continents have ever seen. Watch this space!'

The Chief Lawmaker declared to angry crowds that extra lawkeepers would be sent to each sky whale hotel and that large rewards are available for any information on the identities or whereabouts of the Smog Rats. However, historians suggest that these attacks may signal the beginning of the end for the harmonious Third Age between humans and our sky whale friends. In this new and dangerous age, we must remain vigilant at all times.

ACKNOWLEDGEMENTS

I wrote this story during a time in my life when I needed to write for my own wellbeing. Losing myself in Zeina, Jackson and their world gave me the motivation and confidence to get back to myself. The fact that it has culminated in the publication of *Zeina Starborn and the Sky Whale* is something that still makes me feel like I need to pinch myself and it would not be without a whole host of people who have supported me along the way – so here goes!

The people I feel I must thank first are everyone involved in the Northern Writer's Awards run by New Writing North. I won the Hachette Children's Novel Award in 2020 and this gave me the life-changing opportunity to publish my story with Hachette. Thank you to the lovely judges for seeing the potential in my manuscript, to Will Mackie for guiding me through the very first part of my journey to publication and to everyone at New Writing North for supporting writers in the North of England.

Thank you to my brilliant agent Chloe Seager at the Madeleine Milburn Literary Agency for believing in my story and seeing the potential in me. Thank you for your guidance, kindness and honesty, as well as your patience in the face of my endless queries about publishing! Thank you to the entire Madeleine Milburn team; I feel honoured to be represented by you and so grateful for your expertise and support.

To my incredible editors, Tig Wallace and Nazima Abdillahi at Hachette Children's Group, I cannot thank you enough for all your work in making *Zeina Starborn and the Sky Whale* the story it is today. Thank you for your creativity and kindness while steering me through my first experience of the editorial process. My heartfelt thanks to everyone at Hachette, whether involved at the Award stage, editing, production or promotion and marketing, I truly appreciate your hard work and guidance through every stage of turning my manuscript into a real-life book. It has been an honour to work with you all.

To the extremely talented George Ermos, thank you for my extraordinary cover art, which still makes me cry a little every time I see it. Thank you for bringing Ravenport, Zeina, Jackson and sky whales to life with such beauty and attention to detail.

As well as the amazing people I have met in the book

world, I feel extremely fortunate to have supportive family and friends, without whom *Zeina Starborn and the Sky Whale* would never have been written, let alone read or submitted to anyone.

Thank you to my parents, who passed on their passion for reading and their love of books – a gift that has given me lifelong joy and comfort. My husband for being my biggest champion and always having faith in me even when I had none in myself.

To my daughter, Orla – who is already a marvellous storyteller! – thank you for being my inspiration and motivation and know that you, like Zeina, have the power to change your world. My amazing in-laws who recognised how important writing this story was to me and gave me the time and support to do it. And to (Captain) Heather Parr, a true friend who would make an excellent smog rat.

Thanks to all of you who read any of the (many, many) drafts of this book and provided me with honest but kind feedback or a confidence boost at the times I needed it most.

A special thanks must also go to the Leeds Perinatal Mental Health Service – the professionals that work there and all the amazing women I met there. Thank you for reigniting my love of writing and for giving me the confidence to begin this story.

And finally, thank you to anyone who chooses to read and

support this book. I hope the characters of Zeina and Jackson inspire you to be curious about the world around you, strive to do what you think is right and have the courage to follow your dreams.

Photograph © Declan Creffield

Hannah Durkan is a children's author, whose debut novel, *Zeina Starborn and the Sky Whale,* won the Hachette Children's Novel Award in 2020. She loves writing and reading about fantastical worlds, wonderous adventures and unusual creatures. Hannah grew up in Warwickshire where she enjoyed reading, imagining, exploring and making things out of rubbish. She moved to Yorkshire for university in 2004 and never left. After working as both a doctor and a teacher, Hannah now lives in Leeds with her husband and her two young children, who have finally given her a legitimate excuse for her enormous collection of children's books. When she's not working in a local primary school, she can be found writing stories, drinking coffee, drawing sky whales and making dens.

You can find Hannah on
🐦 @DurkanHannah
📷 @hannahdurkan_author
and on her website at hannahdurkan.co.uk